MORAY

DEATH IN

CW01512345

KATHERINE DALTON RENOIR ('Moray Dalton') was born in Hammersmith, London in 1881, the only child of a Canadian father and English mother.

The author wrote two well-received early novels, *Olive in Italy* (1909), and *The Sword of Love* (1920). However, her career in crime fiction did not begin until 1924, after which Moray Dalton published twenty-nine mysteries, the last in 1951. The majority of these feature her recurring sleuths, Scotland Yard inspector Hugh Collier and private inquiry agent Hermann Glide.

Moray Dalton married Louis Jean Renoir in 1921, and the couple had a son a year later. The author lived on the south coast of England for the majority of her life following the marriage. She died in Worthing, West Sussex, in 1963.

MORAY DALTON MYSTERIES
Available from Dean Street Press

MORAY DALTON

DEATH IN THE CUP

With an introduction by Curtis Evans

DEAN STREET PRESS

LOST GOLD FROM A GOLDEN AGE

The Detective Fiction of Moray Dalton
(Katherine Mary Deville Dalton Renoir, 1881-1963)

"GOLD" COMES in many forms. For literal-minded people gold may be merely a precious metal, physically stripped from the earth. For fans of Golden Age detective fiction, however, gold can be artfully spun out of the human brain, in the form not of bricks but books. While the father of Katherine Mary Deville Dalton Renoir may have derived the Dalton family fortune from nuggets of metallic ore, the riches which she herself produced were made from far humbler, though arguably ultimately mightier, materials: paper and ink. As the mystery writer Moray Dalton, Katherine Dalton Renoir published twenty-nine crime novels between 1924 and 1951, the majority of which feature her recurring sleuths, Scotland Yard inspector Hugh Collier and private inquiry agent Hermann Glide. Although the Moray Dalton mysteries are finely polished examples of criminally scintillating Golden Age art, the books unjustifiably fell into neglect for decades. For most fans of vintage mystery they long remained, like the fabled Lost Dutchman's mine, tantalizingly elusive treasure. Happily the crime fiction of Moray Dalton has been unearthed for modern readers by those industrious miners of vintage mystery at Dean Street Press.

Born in Hammersmith, London on May 6, 1881, Katherine was the only child of Joseph Dixon Dalton and Laura Back Dalton. Like the parents of that admittedly more famous mistress of mystery, Agatha Christie, Katherine's parents hailed from different nations, separated by the Atlantic Ocean. While both authors had British mothers, Christie's father was American and Dalton's father Canadian.

Laura Back Dalton, who at the time of her marriage in 1879 was twenty-six years old, about fifteen years younger than her husband, was the daughter of Alfred and Catherine Mary Back. In her early childhood years Laura Back resided at Valley House, a lovely regency villa built around 1825 in Stratford St. Mary, Suffolk, in the heart of so-called "Constable Country" (so named for the fact that the great Suffolk landscape artist John Constable painted many of his works in and around Stratford). Alfred Back was a wealthy miller who with his brother Octavius, a corn merchant, owned and operated a steam-powered six-story mill right across the River Stour from Valley House. In 1820 John Constable, himself the son of a miller, executed a painting of fishers on the River Stour which partly included the earlier, more modest incarnation (complete with water wheel) of the Back family's mill. (This piece Constable later repainted under the title *The Young Waltonians*, one of his best known works.) After Alfred Back's death in 1860, his widow moved with her daughters to Brondesbury Villas in Maida Vale, London, where Laura in the 1870s met Joseph Dixon Dalton, an eligible Canadian-born bachelor and retired gold miner of about forty years of age who lived in nearby Kew.

Joseph Dixon Dalton was born around 1838 in London, Ontario, Canada, to Henry and Mary (Dixon) Dalton, Wesleyan Methodists from northern England who had migrated to Canada a few years previously. In 1834, not long before Joseph's birth, Henry Dalton started a soap and candle factory in London, Ontario, which after his death two decades later was continued, under the appellation Dalton Brothers, by Joseph and his siblings Joshua and Thomas. (No relation to the notorious "Dalton Gang" of American outlaws is presumed.) Joseph's sister Hannah wed John Carling, a politician who came from a promi- nent family of Canadian brewers and was later knighted for his varied public services, making him Sir John and his wife Lady Hannah. Just how Joseph left the family soap and candle business to prospect for gold is currently unclear, but sometime in the 1870s, after fabulous gold rushes at Cariboo and Cassiar, British Columbia and the Black Hills of South Dakota, among other locales, Joseph left Canada and carried his riches with him to London, England, where for a time he enjoyed life as a gentleman of leisure in one of the great metropolises of the world.

Although Joshua and Laura Dalton's first married years were spent with their daughter Katherine in Ham- mersmith at a villa named Kenmore Lodge, by 1891 the family had moved to 9 Orchard Place in Southampton, where young Katherine received a private education from Jeanne Delport, a governess from Paris. Two decades later, Katherine, now 30 years old, resided with her parents at Perth Villa in the village of Merriott, Somerset, today about an eighty miles' drive west of Southampton. By this time Katherine had published, under the masculine-sounding pseudonym of Moray Dalton (probably a gender-bending play on "Mary Dalton") a well-received first novel, *Olive in Italy* (1909), a study of a winsome orphaned Englishwom- an attempting to make her own living as an artist's model in Italy that possibly had been influenced by E.M. Forster's novels *Where Angels Fear to Tread* (1905) and *A Room with a View* (1908), both of which are partly set in an idealized Italy of pure gold sunlight and passionate love. Yet despite her accomplishment, Katherine's name had no occupation listed next it in the census two years later.

During the Great War the Daltons, parents and child, resided at 14 East Ham Road in Littlehampton, a seaside resort town located 19 miles west of Brighton. Like many other bookish and patriotic British women of her day, Katherine produced an effusion of memorial war poetry, including "To Some Who Have Fallen," "Edith Cavell," "Rupert Brooke," "To Italy" and "Mort Homme." These short works appeared in the *Spectator* and were reprinted during and after the war in George Herbert Clarke's *Treasury of War Poetry* anthologies. "To Italy," which Katherine had composed as a tribute to the beleaguered British ally after its calamitous defeat, at the hands of the forces of Germany and Austria-Hungary, at the Battle of Caporetto in 1917, even popped up in the United States in the "poet's corner" of the *United Mine Workers Journal*, perhaps on account of the poem's pro-Italy sentiment, doubtlessly agreeable to Italian miner immigrants in America.

Katherine also published short stories in various periodicals, including *The Cornhill Magazine*, which was then edited by Leonard Huxley, son of the eminent zoologist Thomas Henry Huxley and father of famed writer Aldous Huxley. Leonard Huxley obligingly read over--and in his words "plied my scalpel upon"--Katherine's second novel, *The Sword of Love*, a romantic adventure saga set in the Florentine Republic at the time of Lorenzo the Magnificent and the infamous Pazzi Conspiracy, which was published in 1920. Katherine writes with obvious affection for *il bel paese* in her first two novels and her poem "To Italy," which concludes with the ringing lines

> Greece was enslaved, and Carthage is but dust,
> But thou art living, maugre [i.e., in spite of] all thy
>   scars,
> To bear fresh wounds of rapine and of lust,
> Immortal victim of unnumbered wars.
> Nor shalt thou cease until we cease to be
> Whose hearts are thine, beloved Italy.

The author maintained her affection for "beloved Italy" in her later Moray Dalton mysteries, which include sympathetically-rendered Italian settings and characters.

Around this time Katherine in her own life evidently discovered romance, however short-lived. At Brighton in the spring of 1921, the author, now nearly 40 years old, wed a presumed Frenchman, Louis Jean Renoir, by whom the next year she bore her only child, a son, Louis Anthony Laurence Dalton Renoir. (Katherine's father seems to have missed these important developments in his daughter's life, apparently having died in 1918, possibly in the flu pandemic.) Sparse evidence as to the actual existence of this man, Louis Jean Renoir, in Katherine's life suggests that the marriage may not have been a successful one. In the 1939 census Katherine was listed as living with her mother Laura at 71 Wallace Avenue in Worthing, Sussex, another coastal town not far from Brighton, where she had married Louis Jean eighteen years earlier; yet he is not in evidence, even though he is stated to be Katherine's husband in her mother's will, which was probated in Worthing in 1945. Perhaps not unrelatedly, empathy with what people in her day considered unorthodox sexual unions characterizes the crime fiction which Katherine would write.

Whatever happened to Louis Jean Renoir, marriage and motherhood did not slow down "Moray Dalton." Indeed, much to the contrary, in 1924, only a couple of years after the birth of her son, Katherine published, at the age of 42 (the same age at which P.D. James published her debut mystery novel, *Cover Her Face*), *The Kingsclere Mystery*, the first of her 29 crime novels. (Possibly the title was derived from the village of Kingsclere, located some 30 miles north of Southampton.) The heady scent of Renaissance romance which perfumes *The Sword of Love* is found as well in the first four Moray Dalton mysteries (aside from *The Kingsclere Mystery*, these are *The Shadow on the Wall*, *The Black Wings* and *The Stretton Darknesse Mystery*), which although set in the present-day world have, like much of the mystery fiction of John Dickson Carr, the elevated emotional temperature of the highly-colored age of the cavaliers. However in 1929 and 1930, with the publication of, respectively, *One by One They Disappeared*, the first of the Inspector Hugh Collier mysteries and *The Body in the Road*, the debut Hermann Glide tale, the Moray Dalton novels begin to become more typical of British crime fiction at that time, ultimately bearing considerable similarity to the work of Agatha Christie and Dorothy L. Sayers, as well as other prolific women mystery authors who would achieve popularity in the 1930s, such as Margery Allingham, Lucy Beatrice Malleson (best known as "Anthony Gilbert") and Edith Caroline Rivett, who wrote under the pen names E.C.R. Lorac and Carol Carnac.

For much of the decade of the 1930s Katherine shared the same publisher, Sampson Low, with Edith Rivett, who published her first detective novel in 1931, although Rivett moved on, with both of her pseudonyms, to that rather more prominent purveyor of mysteries, the Collins Crime Club. Consequently the Lorac and Carnac novels are better known today than those of Moray Dalton. Additionally, only three early Moray Dalton titles (*One by One They Disappeared*, *The Body in the Road* and *The Night of Fear*) were picked up in the United States, another factor which mitigated against the Dalton mysteries achieving long-term renown. It is also possible that the independently wealthy author, who left an estate valued, in modern estimation, at nearly a million American dollars at her death at the age of 81 in 1963, felt less of an imperative to "push" her writing than the typical "starving author."

Whatever forces compelled Katherine Dalton Renoir to write fiction, between 1929 and 1951 the author as Moray Dalton published fifteen Inspector Hugh Collier mysteries and ten other crime novels (several of these with Hermann Glide). Some of the non-series novels daringly straddle genres. *The Black Death*, for example, somewhat bizarrely yet altogether compellingly merges the murder mystery with post-apocalyptic science fiction, whereas *Death at the Villa*, set in Italy during the Second World War, is a gripping wartime adventure thriller with crime and death. Taken together, the imaginative and ingenious Moray Dalton crime fiction, wherein death is not so much a game as a dark and compelling human drama, is one of the more significant bodies of work by a Golden Age mystery writer—though the author has, until now, been most regrettably overlooked by publishers, for decades remaining accessible almost solely to connoisseurs with deep pockets.

Even noted mystery genre authorities Jacques Barzun and Wendell Hertig Taylor managed to read only five books by Moray Dalton, all of which the pair thereupon listed in their massive critical compendium, *A Catalogue of Crime* (1972; revised and expanded 1989). Yet Barzun and Taylor were warm admirers of the author's writing, avowing for example, of the twelfth Hugh Collier mystery, *The Condamine Case* (under the impression that the author was a man): "[T]his is the author's 17th book, and [it is] remarkably fresh and unstereotyped [actually it was Dalton's 25th book, making it even more remarkable—C.E.]. . . . [H]ere is a neglected man, for his earlier work shows him to be a conscientious workman, with a flair for the unusual, and capable of clever touches."

Today in 2019, nine decades since the debut of the conscientious and clever Moray Dalton's Inspector Hugh Collier detective series, it is a great personal pleasure to announce that this criminally neglected woman is neglected no longer and to welcome her books back into light. Vintage crime fiction fans have a golden treat in store with the classic mysteries of Moray Dalton.

TRUTH COMES GLIDING

Moray Dalton's *The Body in the Road* (1930), *The Night of Fear* (1931) and *Death in the Cup* (1932)

In 1928 Agatha Christie, still disheartened and demoralized by a rapid succession of psychic hammer blows-- the recent death of her beloved mother, ongoing marital discord with her estranged husband Archie and her brief though highly publicized and embarrassing "disappearance" of two years earlier--published *The Mystery of the Blue Train*, her fifth Hercule Poirot detective novel and one the Queen of Crime remembered ever after with pronounced distaste. "Really, how that wretched book ever came to be written, I don't know!" she exclaimed with exasperation of *The Blue Train* in her posthumously published Autobiography, composed between 1950 and 1965. "I had no joy in writing, no élan," she recalled of those dismal days, adding bluntly:

> I had worked out the plot—a conventional plot, partly adapted from one of my other stories. I knew, as one might say, where I was going, but I could not see the scene in my mind's eye, and the people would not come alive. I was driven desperately on by the desire, indeed the necessity, to write another book and make some money.
>
> That was the moment when I changed from an amateur to a professional. I assumed the burden of a profession, which is to write even when you don't want to, don't much like what you are writing, and aren't writing particularly well. I have always hated *The Mystery of the Blue Train*, but I got it written,

and sent off to the publishers. It sold just as well as my last book had done.

Not only did the book sell well, but contemporary critical notices of the latest Hercule Poirot murder opus were good and modern mystery readers, obviously not burdened with Christie's emotional baggage, continue to give the novel good marks today. Moreover, whatever one's feelings about the quality of *The Mystery of the Blue Train*, there assuredly is found between its covers at least one notable character (aside from Poirot himself): a certain mysterious individual named Mr. Goby. Early in the novel this enigmatic private inquiry agent is consulted by American millionaire Rufus Van Aldin. (An inordinate number of American millionaires in Golden Age British mysteries seem to have come of Dutch extraction by way of New York, formerly New Netherland.) The demanding tycoon desires to collect dirt on his son-in-law, Derek Kettering, on behalf of his daughter, Ruth, who is planning, with her father's encouragement, to slap her errant husband with a divorce suit. In Chapter Five Mr. Goby is introduced to readers as "a small, elderly man, shabbily dressed, with eyes that looked carefully all around the room, and never at the person he was addressing." After concluding his succinct interview with Mr. Goby, who during the entire time successively gazes at the radiator, the left hand drawer of the desk, the cornice and the fender, but never at his client, a gratified Mr. Van Aldin confidently pronounces to his secretary: "That's a very useful man. . . . In his own line [the sale of information] he's a specialist. Give him twenty-four hours and he would lay the private life of the Archbishop of Canterbury bare for you." Despite his mild appearance, Mr. Goby, one imagines, could have gone toe-to-toe with Dashiell Hammett's private dick The Continental Op, who in novel form debuted the next year in *Red Harvest* (1929).

Despite her later dismissal of the worth of *The Blue Train*, Christie from some corner of her clever mind must have recollected Mr. Goby with gratification, for many years later she revived him in three additional Hercule Poirot mysteries: *After the Funeral* (1953), *Third Girl* (1966) and *Elephants Can Remember* (1972), the latter work the very last Poirot tale that she wrote. Elderly Mr. Goby ultimately enjoyed nearly as great longevity as the brilliant Belgian sleuth himself. Another crime writer upon whom Mr. Goby may have made an impression was Moray Dalton, whose sixth mystery novel, *The Body in the Road* (published in the UK and US in 1930, two years after *The Mystery of the Blue Train*), introduces a Mr. Glide, a Mr. Hermann Glide, who rather resembles Christie's own Mr. Goby. However, Mr. Glide in contrast with Mr. Goby is far from a minor character, being, rather, the man who actually solves the puzzling murders in *The Body in the Road* and two successor novels, *The Night of Fear* (1931) and *Death in the Cup* (1932).

In *The Body in the Road* Mr. Glide is first mentioned nearly four-fifths of the way into the novel. This is after Lord David Chant--formerly an investigator at Scotland Yard but now moodily ensconced at Spinacres, a rural estate in southern England, having against all odds inherited the family title--travels to London to meet with his former superior. Lord David is seeking advice on how to help the legally imperiled young woman whom he holds most dear: Linda Merle, a former piano accompanist in the town of Jessop's Bridge near Spinacres, who shockingly has been charged with the murder of her friend Violet Hunter, the beautiful, blonde and ingenuous violinist whom Linda Merle accompanied at the Tudor Café. Declaring that nothing can be done through official channels to help Lord David and his lady love, David's one-time Chief advises him to seek the aid of Hermann Glide. "I've heard of him," responds Lord David doubtfully of the private inquiry agent. "A bit of a mountebank, isn't he?" To which his Chief judiciously responds: "He is none too scrupulous about the means he employs to attain his ends, though I fancy he is clever enough to keep within the law. . . . we keep in touch with him here. We don't approve of him—but we find him useful."

Ushered into Mr. Glide's office by his loyal secretary, Miss Briggs, Lord David finds seated before him at a shabby desk a "little man, noticeably frail in appearance, with wistful brown eyes in a small puckered face," who rather reminds him of a "monkey on a barrel organ." Although, in contrast with Mr. Goby, Mr. Glide apparently can look his clients evenly in the face, he prefers to devote his surface attention to a lump of modeling wax, which during interviews he molds into "fantastic shapes" with his "long slender supple fingers." Yet Mr. Glide is paying close attention indeed to what Lord David has to tell him, and it is he who engineers a far happier outcome to the case than readers might well have expected when Glide was first consulted by the master of Spinacres, for things then looked very dark indeed for David and Linda. Just how Mr. Glide accomplishes this feat makes an ingenious finish to a most gripping tale of murder, which though primarily a detective novel shares some affinity with the

Golden Age thrillers of Edgar Wallace and Agatha Christie. (Over the course of the novel we observe two characters, both women, reading Edgar Wallace novels.)

A year after the publication of *The Body in the Road*, the perspicacious Mr. Glide reappeared, this time about forty percent of the way into the story, to solve another strange killing in *The Night of Fear*, Moray Dalton's bravura turn on a classic country house Christmas mystery. Family and friends and assorted servants were gathered at Laverne Peveril, home of George Tunbridge and his wife, when bloody murder struck, during what was meant to be a jolly holiday game of hide-and-seek. Evidence points to George's old public school friend Hugh Darrow, but this view is challenged by Inspector Collier, who made his first appearance a couple of years earlier in *One by One They Disappeared* (1929) and within a few years would supersede Hermann Glide as Moray Dalton's primary series sleuth.

The conscientious Scotland Yard inspector happens to be on the scene visiting his friend Sergeant Lane and at Lane's invitation he unofficially participates in the early stages of the investigation. He later briefly takes over the investigation after Lane is sidelined. However, at the behest of George's string-pulling cousin, Sir Eustace Tunbridge, Collier is pulled off the case and replaced by a disliked rival from the Yard, who proceeds to arrest Darrow. At Collier's suggestion, visiting American Ruth Clare, who loves Hugh dearly, turns to Hermann Glide for help—a most fortunate decision, as it transpires.

In 1932 Hermann Glide again arrives to save the day, this time in *Death in the Cup*, an absorbing account of murder in the poisoned bosom of a genteel, if alarmingly dysfunctional, family in Dennyford, a smugly insular provincial town in southern England that a visiting character ironically describes as a "peaceful little place . . . so typically English, almost Jane Austen still in the twentieth century, where the most exciting thing that could happen would be the lowering of somebody's golf handicap. . . ." Mr. Glide appears halfway through the novel, in service of Geoffrey Raynham (lately retired from the East), the concerned uncle of young Lucy Rivers, who is in love with Byronically handsome Mark Armour, the chief suspect of the local police in a most dreadful murder case. An offstage Inspector Collier acts as Glide's and Raynham's go-between.

As the title suggests, both the initial slaying (that of the unhappy Armour family's domineering and blindly unfeeling eldest sister, Bertha) and the one which follows it appear to have been accomplished by means of a poison classically favored by murderers in need: arsenic. Students of English true crime will recollect, as no doubt the author herself did, the unsolved poisonings at Birdhurst Rise, a Victorian villa in Croydon, south London. There between April 1928 and March 1929 a man, his sister-in-law and mother-in-law died most mysteriously, all of them in all likelihood from the ingestion of fatal amounts of arsenic. In contrast with the Croydon poisoning case, however, the killer in *Death in the Cup* is finally collared, with credit going once again to the wit and wiles of wizened Mr. Glide. Surely even Agatha Christie's Mr. Goby could not have put in a more impressive performance than Mr. Glide in these three superb Moray Dalton detective novels.

Curtis Evans

Chapter I
EX-GIGOLO

Two MEN and a woman were sitting together in a corner of a hotel lounge. It was one of the finest hotels on the south coast. A constant stream of traffic flowed past the windows, and, across the road, waves were breaking on the beach.

The woman was stout, elderly, expensively clothed and heavily made up. The men were both young. One, who was addressed as Ken, was slim and fair. He lay back in his chair and appeared to be half asleep while keeping a wary eye on his companions. The other was the possessor of the kind of good looks that are often described as Byronic. In other words he was dark and he looked unhappy.

"So nice of you to look me up," babbled the lady. "What a pity you're still so lame. Mark was my dancing partner, Ken, before he broke his leg. He danced divinely."

"Thank you, Violet," said Mark.

The fair youth yawned. "Badly set, I suppose. What putrid luck." Mark raged inwardly. Why hadn't Violet Lobb got rid of that puppy for the afternoon and seen him alone? Probably because she was not an utter fool and had guessed that he hoped to borrow something to go on with. She would not have missed it, and Heaven knew she had got her money's worth out of him in the past.

Some women who were unwieldy in appearance were light on their feet, he reflected, but Violet was not. Twelve stone to push round the floor night after night, and tea dances two or three afternoons a week. And it had not been easy to keep her in a good temper either.

A waiter approached and Mrs. Lobb ordered tea and went on talking. "I'm off to Cannes next week. Ken booked the places in the Blue train this morning. He's coming, too, to look after my correspondence and so forth. I can't do without a secretary." The diamonds on her fat fingers flashed as she poured out the tea. "Sugar, Mark? I've forgotten. Shall you get over this lameness in time? Look me up again when I get back in April."

She had not meant to say that. It was better to make a clean cut. But he certainly was extraordinarily good looking, and he was not as grasping as some. He had never played up as Ken did. But he was no use to her if he couldn't dance. She must have constant exercise to keep her weight down.

Mark drank his tea and smoked a cigarette. He wondered what she would say if he told her that he got the money for his railway fare to Brighton from his sister Claire, and that he had exactly three halfpence left. She was not the kind of woman whose heart is softened by hard luck stories, and in any case he would rather have died than make any such admission in the hearing of the bored and languid Ken. The latter, meanwhile, was looking at his wrist watch.

"I say, Violet, it's past four. I hear the band tuning up. What about it?"

His patroness nodded. "I'm coming," she said gaily. Mark looked rather miserable, but it was no good being silly and sentimental about him. She turned to him, holding out her podgy hand. "So sweet of you to come over. Good-bye and good luck," she said.

The fair youth smiled. "Cheerio, Armour."

Mrs. Lobb hoisted herself up and waddled away, her escort following carrying her fur wrap, her gold chain bag, and her novel.

Mark Armour stared after them for a moment before he picked up his hat and passed out through the revolving doors to meet the cold wind blowing in from the sea.

Three halfpence and the return half of his ticket from Dennyford. He would have to catch the next train home. He would have to go back to hear Winnie's foolish giggle, poor old George munching his food, and Bertha's incessant nagging. Claire had borne it all these years, and he had only been home a few weeks and had reached the limits of endurance. But women, he supposed, were more patient. His position at home was degrading, humiliating, impossible. But there was no way out of it without money, and he could not think of any means of earning a livelihood.

When he changed into the branch line train at the junction he saw Lucy Rivers' aunt with another woman getting into the compartment next to his. Miss Rivers was tall, upright, and grey-haired. She knew him, of course, by sight, but they were not on bowing terms. He wondered what she would say if he told her that her niece had promised to meet him that night at eleven in the last shelter along the parade. He could hear the murmur of her voice and her friend's. Probably they were talking about him. For years past the Armours had supplied Dennyford with an unfailing topic of conversation. The scandals about them had begun, Mark supposed, when his father married his mother, who was his children's French governess, only three weeks after his first wife's death. There had been plenty of others since to enliven the local tea parties and keep the family outside the social pale. The result had been that while everybody knew of the Armours nobody went near them, except, very occasionally, to ask for subscriptions.

The White House was a mile outside the town. A bus passed the gate every hour, but the fare was threepence so that Mark was obliged to walk.

He had left the town behind him and was approaching the bridge over the railway cutting. There were fields on either hand. On the right were two thatched cottages that had been there since 1690, the date carved over the lintel, and on the left a row of tall stuccoed houses of which only one was occupied. They had been derelict for some time and were to let at very low rents. The end house had been taken as a rather forlorn hope by a young doctor who had put up a brass plate and was trying to work up a practice. Claire Armour had been to him for a whitlow and her report had been favourable. He was painstaking, she said, and moderate in his fees, especially if his patients came to him in his surgery hours. He was a Scot and his name was Cardew, Ian Cardew.

Mark, whose leg was aching rather badly by the time he reached Victoria Terrace, yielded to an impulse to call on the doctor and get his opinion. He rang the bell but there was no reply. There was a faint light in the hall. He rang again and then turned the door handle and walked in.

The door of the surgery was open. He entered and sat down to wait. He had been there about ten minutes when the doctor hurried in.

He was a big-boned, gaunt-looking young man with freckles and red hair.

"Sorry to keep you waiting. A little fool of a skivvy nearly sliced her hand off with a bread knife I had to put in five stitches, and it took longer than I expected. My housekeeper's down in the basement and as deaf as a post. What can I do for you?" Mark explained. "I broke my leg last June. It was a bad break and they had to cut out a splinter of bone. I want to know if I shall always be lame."

"Let's have a look at it."

Ian Cardew's manner was against him but he was a competent surgeon and his big red hands worked swiftly and without fumbling.

"Yes," he said at last. "They made the best job they could of it. Do you want the truth?"

"Yes."

"Then I think that in time there'll be no pain, but you'll always walk with a limp."

"I see. Thank you. Do you mind if I pay you what I owe to-morrow?"

"That's all right," said Cardew brusquely. "I don't know your name."

"My name is Armour. I live at the White House just over the railway bridge."

"Oh—I hadn't realised—"

They were in the narrow hall-way by this time. Someone had pushed a note through the letter box while they were in the surgery. It was lying on the mat and Mark stooped instinctively to pick it up. As he handed it to Cardew he saw and recognised the weak sprawling handwriting with a shock of distaste. So Winnie was corresponding with the doctor. He glanced at the young man's flushed face and pitied him. He was probably only at the beginning of his troubles, for Winnie had the terrifying persistence of her type. Venus *toute entière a sa proi attachée.* In other words, she stuck like a limpet. "Well, anyhow I won't bilk him," he thought. There was a wardrobe dealer in the town and he might get a few shillings for one of his suits, or there was the platinum cigarette case that South American woman had given him the winter before last. She was freer with her money than Mrs. Lobb.

He said good night and limped away down the road in the gathering dusk, the fallen leaves rustling under his feet.

CHAPTER II
FIVE IN FAMILY

BERTHA WAS BULLYING Winnie in the dining-room. She was not angry without a cause, for she had just had a letter signed Ian Cardew begging her to cease writing to him, "as no good purpose could be served by further correspondence." Obviously this appeal was meant for Winnie and had been addressed to her by mistake.

"I'm ashamed of you," said Bertha icily. "You make me sick."

Bertha was nearly fifty and looked her age. Her figure had spread and her sandy hair was growing thin. She dressed sensibly in woollen jumpers and homespun tweeds. She had a strident voice and was given to finding fault. The maids hated her, but the house was well run, spotlessly clean, and the meals were well cooked and punctually served. She was a good manager, but the human element in her own family defeated her.

"You promised me last year that this sort of thing wouldn't happen again," she said for about the fifth time.

"You don't understand. I love him so—" wailed Winnie. Shakily she produced a handkerchief with a torn lace edge and blew her nose. She sat hunched up in her chair, moist and flabby, her weak little face blotched with crying.

"Rubbish. Do try to control yourself. For Heaven's sake stop sniffing!" Bertha clenched her hands. She often felt tempted to shake her sister. "I shall answer this letter. I intend to ask Doctor Cardew to let me know if he has any further trouble with you. If he has to complain again I shall take steps."

"Steps—" faltered Winnie.

"Steps!" shouted Bertha. "I shall have you certified. So now you know!"

George was in the little room on the ground floor that had been given up to him. He had a patch of ground in the garden where he dug and sowed seeds, but most of his time was spent indoors. He had only one occupation, but that never failed him. He cut pictures out of illustrated papers and pasted them into albums.

Claire, passing by the window, glanced in and saw his placid bearded face bent as usual over his self-appointed task. She knocked on the pane and held up her basket of windfallen apples for his inspection. He stared vacantly for a moment and then smiled. He preferred his half-sister to either Bertha or Winnie.

Claire went in by the back door and put the apples in the larder. The cook and housemaid, seeing her, left the foot of the kitchen stairs where they had been listening to the raised voices in the dining-room. "Another row," thought Claire wearily. She met her brother Mark on the landing.

"I didn't know you'd come back."

"I haven't been back long."

"Did you have a good time?"

He had borrowed the money for his fare to Brighton from her. She had understood that he had an invitation from friends. She was his only confidante but he did not tell her much.

"A good time? No, a hell of a time. Hark at Bertha jawing the wretched Winnie. It's sheer cruelty. The woman can't help being a fool."

"I'm afraid Winnie has started another pash," said Claire. "She's beginning to dress up. That's always a bad sign. That wisp of blue chiffon she ties round her neck. She had it on this morning."

"It's that doctor chap over the bridge." Mark related what had happened. "She'd dropped a note through the letter box."

"I suppose Bertha has found out. Oh, dear," sighed Claire. "Winnie was kind to me when I was in bed with flu last winter. She nursed me day and night. Bertha never came near me. She said I must pull myself together and that the maids had enough to do without carrying up my meals. Winnie did everything for me and made no fuss. Bertha's as hard as nails."

"Don't I know it!" said Mark bitterly. "I hate her. Her voice gets on my nerves. It's worse every day. I can't imagine how you've stuck it all these years."

"Look out. There's somebody coming upstairs. Oh, it's Gladys with the hot water."

The Armours dined at half-past seven. Since their father's death Bertha had taken the head of the table, dispensing the soup and carving the joint. George, Mark and Claire were present, but Gladys brought a message from Winnie. She was lying down with a headache and did not want anything to eat.

A roast loin of pork followed the artichoke soup and fried soles.

Bertha ate heartily of every course. She always enjoyed her food. She thought of going to that new fishmonger that had just opened down the High Street. She had seen lemon soles there for twopence a pound less than Barney had charged her. "The profiteering that goes on is simply disgraceful. It's the fault of the Government. If I had my way—"

Mark was silent. He neither agreed nor disagreed. Bertha's conversation bored him and he tried not to listen. He would borrow another shilling from Claire after dinner and catch the last bus, the 8.35 into Dennyford. Claire was cutting up George's meat for him. Though he did not mind scissors he had a horror of knives and always ate with a spoon. George, of course, did not count. Often days passed without his uttering a word. Gladys, the house-parlourmaid, moved noiselessly about the room, a black and white robot changing plates and taking dishes from the service hatch. The harsh white glare of the incandescent gas burners was merciless to the ugly Victorian clumsy furniture, the sideboard, the heavy steel fireirons and fender, the engravings after Landseer that hung on the walls. Four meals a day. Three hundred and sixty-five days in the year. Bertha finished her last morsel of cheese and got up from the table.

"I wish you'd see George to bed to-night, Mark. I have to write a letter."

"Very well."

George could undress himself, but he had to have his light turned out for him when he was safe in bed, and someone to hear his childish prayers.

Mark, standing by the bedroom door, waited with suppressed impatience. It was no use trying to hurry George. He did everything at a snail's pace.

At last he was ready, and Mark turned out the gas and hurried off to find Claire.

She was not in her room and he was still looking for her when he heard the bus passing the gate. There wasn't another and he would have to walk. There was a ground mist but it was not cold. The scent of the bonfire the gardener had made earlier in the day lingered, mingled with the autumnal smell of dead leaves and rotting apples.

As he passed down the drive to the gate Mark caught a glimpse of two shadowy figures, rapt and motionless, half hidden by the laurels. Gladys with one of her followers—but had she finished clearing away?

Mark drew a long breath. His spirits were rising. He felt younger as he limped briskly down the road and looked up at the stars. It was a still night and he could hear the waves breaking on the beach a mile away. It was such a blessed relief to get away from the family for an hour or two. Claire was all right, and he could stand poor old George and even Winnie but, God! how he hated Bertha with her querulous fault-finding and her self-complacency. That voice of hers going on and on like a rasping saw until he wanted to stop his ears or rush out of the room. "That'll do," he told himself, "forget it!" And he thought instead of the last shelter on the long deserted sea front where Lucy would meet him and they would sit together making love while the sea, unseen in the darkness, stirred gently like some sleeping animal and lipped the shelving beach, and the gulls floated placidly with the falling tide farther and farther away.

CHAPTER III

UNDER THE ROSE

"THAT YOUNGER BROTHER of Miss Armour's was in the train coming back from Brighton," said Miss Rivers as she stood with her niece in the drawing-room after dinner waiting for her brother who, as usual, had mislaid his glasses. They were going round to the Lawsons to play bridge. "He walks very lame, but he certainly is phenomenally good looking. A perfect profile, which is so unusual. Thin as a lath, which saves him from being a barber's block, and very dark. Rather like a handsome gipsy." She appealed to Colonel Rivers who had just come. "Was old Armour's second wife a gipsy, John?"

"No. French. French governess to his elder children. I wonder if that son of hers has come home for good. I've seen him hanging about."

"It seems a pity a young man like that should have nothing to do," said Miss Rivers.

"Lawson told me once that he was going into the bank years ago, but there was some fuss about the old man's signature on a cheque passed by the boy. He wasn't seen in Dennyford for years after that. Not, in fact, until recently. I should say he was a complete rotter. The whole family is impossible and outside the pale. If you are ready, Mary, I am."

"Quite." Miss Rivers patted her untidy shock of iron grey hair and wound a scarf round her neck. "You won't sit up for us, Lucy, of course. I don't suppose we shall be back much before one. I should go early if I were you, dear. You look rather tired."

"All right, Auntie."

Dutifully Lucy kissed her aunt and her father and went with them to the door, waiting until she heard the click of the garden gate before she returned to the drawing-room. Her heart was thumping against her ribs. She noticed how her hands were shaking as she stood by the piano turning over her music. Parker came in. The Rivers kept two maids but they both went home at night.

"Any letters for me to post, Miss?"

"No, thank you, Parker."

"I'll be going now if that's all, Miss."

"Good night, Parker."

"Good night, Miss."

Lucy lit a cigarette and smoked half of it. It would never do to be there before him. It would be ghastly to seem too eager. She must not let him know how terribly she cared.

She went up to her room and looked at herself in the glass. At school the other girls had said she was like Botticelli's Flora, and her dearest friend had given her a medici print of the picture. It hung now over her chest of drawers, and she was rather proud of the resemblance, but the fact remained that the Flora was not really pretty. She had not minded so much before but now she deplored her smooth, fine, honey-coloured hair, her noticeably high cheekbones and her pointed chin. Her eyes, she thought, were too pale. "I don't know what he sees in me!" she said aloud despairingly. She wondered if she should change into her green velvet frock, and discovered that it was later than she had thought and that she would not have time. She put on her fur coat. It had been chilly last night on the sea side of the shelter. She made sure that she had her latchkey and ran downstairs and out of the house.

Simla was at the far end of the Marine Parade and to reach the last shelter she had only to cross the road and to walk a hundred yards to the end of the esplanade. There were sandhills beyond, covered with coarse grass and sea holly and patches of tamarisk, and an old derelict barn.

As she reached the shelter a tall figure rose to meet her. "Darling!"

"Oh, Mark!"

"Look here," he said hurriedly, "there's another couple on the other side. They may be able to overhear us. Won't you come down on the beach?"

Lucy hesitated. It was very dark down there, and that phrase, "another couple," jarred a little. It seemed to bring them down to the level of the shop boys and girls one tried to avoid looking at sprawling behind the groynes or in the fields on Sunday afternoons. Mark was quick to feel the lowering of the emotional temperature. "Just as you like, of course," he said humbly. "It's so divinely kind of you to come at all. If you only knew—I've been in hell, wondering if you'd change your mind."

She glanced through the glass at the pair on the other seat. They seemed absorbed in one another, but the idea of sharing of the shelter with them did not appeal to her. "All right," she whispered, "the beach—but not far down."

"We can sit on the stones with our backs to the wall." He helped her down and sat with his arm around her and her smooth fair head on his shoulder.

"Your hair smells nice, Lucy. It smells of flowers."

"Does it?" she said drowsily. Her feet were cold, but the rest of her was warm. She lifted her face in the darkness and he leant down to her and rubbed his cheek gently against hers.

"Darling! Darling!"

"Darling!" she murmured back.

"Are you happy?"

"Yes."

There was no past and no future, only the present. She was like a swimmer plunging at midnight into a warm, summer sea, floating with closed eyes, soothed, quiescent. Mark, aware of her mood, did nothing to break the spell.

At last she moved and sighed. "I must not stay too long."

"Will you meet me again to-morrow?"

"I can't to-morrow. Some people are coming. Bridge and music. Damn. Oh, Mark, I wish we could meet in an ordinary way!"

"Isn't this good enough?"

"You know what I mean. It seems so unfair"—she thought of what her aunt and her father had said. Whatever had happened in the past, she told herself, Mark had not been to blame. The rest of the family might be as queer as they said, but he was different. Still she felt the need of reassurance. She wished he would tell her a little more about himself, but always when she asked questions he eluded her. "But we can't go on like this," she thought, like drug addicts sunk in delicious torpor and strange ecstasies.

"Mark, before your accident, did you live in London?"

He was stroking the palm of her hand with his forefinger. She thrilled to his touch but she persisted. "Your job was in London?"

"Well, sometimes. It depended on my employers. I was engaged"—the pause was imperceptible—"as a kind of secretary. Sometimes a kind of chauffeur. General utility."

"Then I suppose you'll be going back."

"I don't know. I shall have to find something. It isn't easy. The market's glutted. But I can't stand it here much longer. If it wasn't for you, Lucy."

"Oh, Mark!"—she had not been prepared for such concentrated bitterness. "I love you," she whispered.

"My sweet."

She would have given him her lips, but now he held her from him. He had been drifting with her. She had brought him back to earth.

Earth, he thought despairingly. A lee shore. "Look here, Lucy," he forced himself to go on, "I ought not to let you do this. I—I—anyone will tell you—I'm a rotter—no use at all. Living from hand to mouth. Not a chance of anything better. I've a roof over my head and free meals as long as I toe the line. A dog with a bad name. I love you, Lucy. I'd die for you. God! that ought to be easy. Life's no great catch. But I can't—I can't." His voice broke.

He felt her fingers clinging closer to his as she whispered back:

"You mean you can't—ask me to marry you?"

"Yes."

"Never mind. Don't worry, Mark, darling. We'll just go on loving. Perhaps something will turn up. Don't be so unhappy."

It was she now who drew his head down to her breast. Neither spoke for a while. Lucy sat listening to the unchanging, eternal rhythm of the waves breaking on the beach, the oncoming rush, the slow withdrawal. Her heart ached, but she was thinking. "I shall look back on this. I wouldn't have missed it."

They were roused by the striking of the Town Hall clock. Mark sat up. "Twelve! I'd no idea it was so late! Will you be able to get in?"

"Yes. Daddie and Aunt Mary are out playing bridge. They won't be back yet. But I'd better go."

"Shall I see you as far as your gate?"

"Better not. Mark—if you like I'll meet you again Friday night."

"Don't, Lucy. Forget me."

They clung together for a moment silently. Then she slipped out of his arms and was gone.

The house was in darkness when she reached it, but she knew that at any moment now Colonel Rivers and his sister might return. Hastily she slipped out of her clothes and crept into bed. If Aunt Mary looked in she would pretend to be asleep. Poor Aunt Mary. Fancy being like that, thought Lucy, filled with a young contempt and a young pity for the frustration and sterility of the older generation. Wasn't it better to be miserable—and alive—as she was.

"But, oh, Mark, I want you."

She cried herself to sleep.

CHAPTER IV

THE CAPTIVES SET FREE

DOCTOR CARDEW was awakened by the bell that rang beside his bed. He looked at his watch as he switched on the light. Twenty minutes past four. It was still dark, but he could hear cocks crowing in distant farm yards. He got out of bed and leaned out of the window.

"Who is it?"

"Miss Pierce, housemaid at the White House. Will you please come at once? Miss Armour is ill. She's very bad."

Cardew's heart sank for he thought she meant Winnie. Had he made a mistake in writing so strong a letter? With that unbalanced hysterical type one never knew. She might have attempted suicide.

"All right," he said. "Wait for me. I'll be down in three minutes."

He hurried into his clothes, fetched his bag from the surgery, and joined the girl on the doorstep. They walked up the road together under the fading stars. She was excited and voluble.

"Miss Claire came and asked cook to get up and light the fire to get some hot water for a bottle and poultices. She was as white as a sheet herself, poor thing, and when the door was opened it gave me quite a turn to hear the retching. If you ask me I'd say it was the pork. She's a hearty feeder, and she had two helpings. I thought to myself at the time: 'Rather you than me!' I do hope she's quieter now. A noise like that is upsetting."

There were lights in all the lower windows of the White House, and the hall door stood open. Claire, in a faded blue kimono, came down the stairs to meet them.

"I saw you from the landing window. Cook is with her. She seems a little easier, but the strain has been terrible. It's been going on over an hour. And she's gone a funny colour. Thank you, Gladys. Will you see that the kitchen fire is all right? And you might make some tea. Will you come up now, doctor?"

Cardew followed her into the sick room, and there his first sensation was one of relief, for the woman on the bed was not Winnie Armour. All right, he thought; all right.

She hasn't tried to score off me by killing herself. This was an older, stouter woman, with no trace of poor Winnie's faded prettiness, lying with closed eyes, exhausted.

He felt her pulse. It was barely perceptible.

The slow hours passed. Breakfast was late and only three of the family came down for it. George, staring bewildered at the unaccustomed sight of Winnie pouring out tea at the head of the table; Mark with weary eyes and lips compressed; Winnie, twittering, with sidelong glances, blinking nervously at them both as she fumbled over the cups. Afterwards George shuffled silently back to his scrap album, and Winnie went to sit in the drawing-room with the door open, waiting to waylay Cardew when he came down. They couldn't say she was running after him, she told herself, if she just asked how Bertha was. It would look very strange if she took no notice.

Mark lingered too, but on the upper landing. Claire joined him presently. Her dark face was grey with fatigue.

Cardew, emerging from the sick room a few minutes later, saw them standing together by the landing window. Mark turned to him at once. "How is she?"

"Easier just now. But she should have a trained nurse. I must go home now and I will ring up for one. I'll come back as soon as I can. You will have to stay with her meanwhile, Miss Armour. Have the cook with you. She seems a sensible woman. I'm sorry it all devolves on you."

"Oh, poor Winnie would be terrified. I'll do my best. Thank you, Doctor." Claire hesitated an instant. "I suppose she has got over the worst?"

"I can't say that. I hope so. But she is very weak." He looked over the banisters into the hall below and saw the drawing-room door standing open and a glimpse of Winnie's blue jumper.

"Are there any back stairs?"

"Yes. Here."

Mark turned to his sister when the doctor had gone. "He's not over civil."

"He's tired and worried," said Claire, excusing him. "I wonder why he's gone into the kitchen. I can hear him talking to the cook."

"He oughtn't to do that," said Mark irritably. "He's a bit of a bounder, I fancy. Breakfast was ghastly with Winnie pouring out. Can I do anything to help?"

"I don't think so."

"Then I'll make myself scarce."

Claire returned to the sick room and found the patient dozing. She was joined almost immediately by the cook, who announced that the doctor had said that the nurse would arrive about eleven.

"And until then, Miss, I'm to stay up here with you."

"Thank you, Emily," said Claire coldly. She did not like the cook. They sat without exchanging a word until the nurse came and ousted them both. Cardew returned at noon.

"Any more vomiting?"

"Not since I've been here. She's been ever so quiet."

The young Scotsman's freckled face was very grave. "Her pulse is hardly perceptible. Ring the bell, Nurse."

The nurse obeyed. "Tell the maid, when she comes, to fetch her brothers and sisters."

"Is she—?"

"I'm afraid so."

Claire came in. "Winnie has a horror of illness," she explained. "And Mark is out."

"Out?"

"There didn't seem to be anything for him to do," said Claire. "Is she—worse?"

They made way for her to approach the bedside. She moved forward reluctantly and stood looking down at the ravaged face on the pillow. Yesterday Bertha had been her brusque and self-sufficient self, loud-voiced, dogmatic, she who must be obeyed. Now that solid body had crashed, and with it her mind. Or—had it? Her eyes as they opened were not vacant. They were merely puzzled. As Claire leant over her they fixed themselves with a peculiar intentness on her face. The pale lips moved but made no intelligible sound.

Claire shrank back and the nurse took her place. There was a long minute of silence. Claire heard her own breathing, the nurse's, the doctor's. She did not hear Bertha's.

At last. "I'm sorry," said Cardew.

Mark came in at four o'clock, tired and hungry, from a long solitary tramp across country. He found Claire having tea in the drawing-room; a fire larger than Bertha would have approved blazed in the grate, and the stable kitten was curled up, purring, on the hearthrug.

"You seem comfortable here," said Mark. "Where's everybody? How's Bertha?"

His sister looked at him curiously. "Didn't you notice that the blinds in front were drawn? She died this morning just after twelve."

"Bertha! Dead! I always thought she'd outlive us all. It seems impossible."

Claire sighed. "I feel as if this day had lasted years. I'm afraid Doctor Cardew thought it rather funny of you to go for a walk as if it was just any day, Mark. I told him you didn't realise how ill she was. We none of us did. It was a shock, though I can't pretend I was fond of her. Winnie cried dreadfully and had to be given sal volatile and put to bed. I haven't said anything to George. Gladys took his tea in to him. I didn't feel equal to having a sit down meal with him in the dining-room. Cook suggested lighting a fire in here. She's been very decent and so has Gladys. Of course, in a way, they've enjoyed themselves."

Mark drew a chair nearer and sat down to drink his tea. "What about the funeral?"

"Doctor Cardew is seeing about everything for us. The nurse was here and did what had to be done. An ambulance came half an hour ago and took her away."

"The nurse?"

"No. Bertha. Doctor Cardew told me he wasn't prepared to give a certificate. He said we had better keep everything we had left over from dinner last night. He told the cook in front of me."

"I suppose that means he thinks it may have been food poisoning?"

"I suppose so," she said dully.

He glanced at her weary face. "Poor old Claire! Cardew's an interfering ass. We should have been ill too. We all had the same food. Does the law allow him to take her away and make all this fuss without consulting us?"

She had been leaning back with closed eyes. She opened them to look at him. "Better be careful, Mark. It doesn't matter what you say to me, but don't let anyone else get the idea that you object to a full enquiry."

She noticed that his hand shook slightly as he set down his cup.

"What the hell do you mean?"

"Only this. Doctor Cardew was very stiff with me. He seemed thoroughly uncomfortable, trying to avoid my eye. I don't know what he imagined or suspected, but one can't help guessing. I—I daresay you don't know, but she always had a glass of milk by her bedside to sip at if she woke in the night. She—she was fussy and took great care of herself. After she died, when the room was being made tidy I noticed it wasn't there. I asked the cook and she told me she had meant to take the glass down to be washed but the doctor wouldn't let her, and I think he must have carried it off in his bag. I suppose if there is an inquest—"

"What a thrill for Dennyford!" said Mark. "I can imagine the buzz of conversation. My dear, that dreadful family! Another scandal was about due"—he came back to the hearth and stood gazing moodily down into the red heart of the fire. "They can't prove anything," he muttered.

She glanced anxiously at the beautiful brooding face. She loved her brother, but during the years that had passed since he left home they had grown apart, and she felt instinctively that there was much in his life that he had hidden from her.

"Poor Bertha!" she said with a shudder, recalling the dead woman's long drawn out agony. "If one could only go back a few hours."

"You're tired out," he said, "that's what it is. It'll be all right. I expect Bertha had some internal trouble. She was too stout to be healthy and she was a bad colour. Probably her heart was wrong. What you need, Claire, is a change from this place, and you'll be able to have one now."

"Yes," she murmured, "yes. If I could only believe it! But I feel that something will stop us even now. I'm—I daresay it's silly—but I'm horribly frightened. It's true my nerves are upset. I've had a lot to worry me lately. You'll have to wear a mourning band on your sleeve, Mark, and poor old George, too. I'll go and get my work basket."

Chapter V
SUPERINTENDENT BRISLING

"Auntie, I want to get up."

"Nonsense!" Miss Rivers, very upright and determined, stood by her niece's bed. "You've got a troublesome cough—I heard you in the night—and a temperature, and you'll stay where you are for the present. I'm going into the town to get you a bit of fish for lunch and change the books, but I shan't be long. Ring if you want anything."

She leant over the bed and gave Lucy one of the hard little pecks that, with her, passed for kisses. Lucy tried to smile. She was fond of her aunt. When she was alone her eyes filled with tears. How was she to let Mark know that she could not meet him on the beach to-night? He would wait and wait, and he might think she was a coward, afraid to come. She might write a note, but she would have to trust one of the servants to post it, and she dared not do that. He might worry, and there was nothing to worry about, really. She had caught a cold. "And if I went," she thought, "he'd probably catch it!"

She ate some of the grapes her aunt had left on the table beside her bed. Her throat was dry and she felt hot and uncomfortable. After a while she dozed a little. Miss Rivers was gone some time.

When she came into her niece's room she was still wearing her outdoor things and laden with parcels.

"The girl at Boots' recommended this book for you, and I've brought you some lozenges. That nice man in the chemist's department recommended them. He was so sorry to hear you had a cold. Cook is going to steam the fish. I met Mrs. Lawson and we went into the Orange Tree Café for coffee. It's been redecorated. My dear, what do you think she told me! The eldest Miss Armour died suddenly yesterday. There's going to be an inquest. Just fancy! Why, I saw her outside the butcher's only two days ago. I wonder how they'll get on without her. She looked very disagreeable, but I never heard anything against her. Have you had a little sleep, dear? That's right. Parker will bring up your lunch."

Colonel Rivers came into the dining-room after the gong had sounded. He had been playing golf. He began by enquiring after his daughter.

"How's Lucy?"

"Her temperature is still up, so I'm keeping her in bed. Just a cold, John. Nothing to worry about. You've heard about Miss Armour?" she said eagerly.

She often said that she hated gossip, but Dennyford was a quiet little place, and when a thing like this happened one could not help taking an interest. The Colonel was agreeably titillated too.

"Yes. The man I was playing with told me. Very sudden. I wonder how it will affect the rest of the family."

"How do you mean?"

"The old man left everything to her, you know, but only for her life. I suppose it will be divided equally now. Well, Parker, what is it?" He took the proffered card. "Brisling? Dear me. Show him into the study. I'll come. Go on with your lunch, Mary."

The local superintendent of police was a fresh-complexioned, thick-set man with a pleasant manner and steady blue eyes. He was a hard worker himself and had the knack of getting the best out of his subordinates, but he lacked imagination.

"Sorry to disturb you at lunch time," he said. "I hope Miss Rivers and the young lady are quite well?"

"Quite," said the Colonel, rather surprised at this display of interest. "You didn't come to enquire after them, did you?"

"No, sir. It was just a civil question."

Rivers laughed. "Quite. They're very fit, thanks. At least, Lucy is in bed with a chill. What can I do for you? Sit down, won't you? Have a cigar?"

"Thanks. I'll smoke it later, if you don't mind. The fact is I want you to sign a warrant. I want to have it in case a certain person tries to make a bolt for it."

"A certain person? I don't like mysteries, Brisling."

"Well—I mean young Armour. But I may never serve it, Colonel. I just don't want to be caught napping."

"But Good Heavens! What for?"

"The inquest on his sister opens this afternoon. I'm on my way to it now. We are going to ask for an adjournment, but it's just possible that enough may come out now to justify our making an arrest."

"Good Heavens!" said the Colonel again. "Are you suggesting that he—that she—"

"I'd rather not say very much, but the doctor who was called in, a young fellow who came here a couple of years ago, wasn't satisfied. She had been ill with terrible fits of vomiting for an hour or more before he was fetched by a servant girl in the early hours of the morning. He did what he could—apparently it wasn't much—and was present when she died some hours later. He took possession of a glass that had contained milk that was standing on her bedside table. He noticed some white sediment in it. When he got home he rang us up. I sent one of my men, Collins, round to hear what the servants had to say, and he learned from the cook that she had been awakened between one and two by somebody moving about on the floor below, and that, looking over the banisters, she had seen Mark Armour, fully dressed, just entering his room. She returned to bed and to sleep. It was not until nearly four that she was called by the younger sister to help with Miss Armour."

"Lots of harmless things leave a white sediment."

Brisling nodded. "Patterson carried out the post-mortem, being the police surgeon, and some organs have been sent to the Crown Analyst with the glass. Meanwhile Patterson himself has made some tests and his conclusions agree with those of the doctor who attended her."

"You mean—?"

"Arsenic, Colonel Rivers, and a thundering big dose."

"Shocking!" said the Colonel. "Dear me! Dear me! And he'll be brought before the local Bench, of course. Before us. A terrible responsibility. But he may not have done it, Brisling. You can't be sure. You can't rule out accident or suicide. You'll have to get a lot more evidence before you arrest anyone on such a charge."

"We shall go slow," said Brisling. "Meanwhile, if you'd just sign this warrant."

The Colonel tugged at his white moustache. "No," he said. "I won't sign it. Not yet. You might have known I'd loathe this job. Why did you come to me?"

Brisling said nothing.

The Colonel stared at him. "Gad! I believe you've been to some of my fellow magistrates and that they've declined."

Brisling answered, unabashed, "I tried two as a matter of fact. I'll admit they were unwilling, as you are. It doesn't really matter at this stage. He can't get away, and, as you say, we've got to find out a lot more before we rope in our man. I'll be getting a move on. The enquiry opens at two and our coroner doesn't like to be kept waiting." He looked back from the door. "All this is in confidence, Colonel."

"Naturally. And I hope—I don't know what to hope!" said Rivers. "It's a bad business."

"You can hope we shall find a note left by the deceased to say she was tired of life and meant to do herself in," suggested Brisling; "that would be nice for the survivors. But it isn't very likely. Good morning, Colonel."

CHAPTER VI

FOR THE LAST TIME

"WELL, MY DEAR, how are you?"

"Better, Auntie."

"Is the book I brought you any good?"

"Quite nice."

"Well, now," Miss Rivers stood by the bedside, mechanically patting the eiderdown and breaking off in the middle of a sentence to pick a bit of fluff off the carpet. "I told that girl to come in and take up the pieces. I was sure you wouldn't mind."

"I'm afraid I did," said Lucy apologetically, "she worried me. I told her to leave it."

"Dear me! I hope you aren't getting nervy. Well, I mustn't blame her then. The question is will you mind being left alone in the house this evening while we are at the Millers'?"

Lucy's heart began to thump. She had thought her aunt would insist on giving up her bridge. "Not a bit!" she said eagerly. "I shall be perfectly all right. Absolutely."

"Well, if you're quite sure. You know how difficult it is to make up a four at the last minute, though the Millers would understand if I explained."

"I shall be quite happy. I've got this book, and I can switch off my light and go to sleep when I feel like it."

"Very well," but Miss Rivers glanced doubtfully at her niece's flushed cheeks. "I wonder if I ought to take your temperature again though."

"No. It's gone down. Really. I'll be up tomorrow."

"We shall see. Then I'll tell your father," said her aunt more cheerfully. "Will this dress do if I wear my velvet coat, Lucy?"

"Quite, I think."

"Then I'll say good night. I'll take a peep at you when we come in, but you'll be asleep, I hope."

"Good night, Auntie dear."

How easy it was to deceive them, thought Lucy. They looked upon her still as a little girl. Poor dears. They could never understand. She lay with the bed clothes drawn up to her chin listening until she heard the closing of the front door and the click of the garden gate before she slipped out of bed and began to dress. She was really much better though her throat still felt sore. She would wear a woollen scarf and her fur coat and then she would be all right.

It was a dark night with a fine rain falling that blurred the street lamps, and the parade was deserted as Lucy crossed the road and hurried over to the shelter. Mark was there before her, and rose to meet her. For an instant she had hardly recognised him for he was wearing an overcoat with the collar turned up.

He saw and misunderstood her hesitation. "All right," he said harshly, "go back now if you like. It would be better. I shan't blame you. Goodbye!"

"Mark—"

Something in her voice enlightened him. "Lucy darling. Forgive me. I'm a beast. Come and sit down. We've got this place to ourselves to-night, thank God!" He drew her down on his knees and held her close, burying his face in her fur collar.

"Mark"—she kissed the top of his head—"I heard this morning about Miss Armour. It must have been an awful shock to you all. So sudden. Will it—make a difference to you?"

"Yes. She was my father's favourite. He left us all dependent on her. But she only had a life interest. The estate will be divided now, I believe."

There was a silence. Lucy sat trembling a little in his arms. She felt dazed. Love, to-night, was a drug for them both. The sea murmured to them drowsily in the darkness.

"I mustn't stay long, Mark."

"I won't keep you. But don't go before you must. It's been pretty ghastly, and it isn't over. The funeral's to-morrow."

"I'm sorry. I suppose you were fonder of her than you realised."

"No. I hated her."

She was too shocked to answer him and he hurried on. "I'll never lie to you, Lucy. I hated her—but don't believe—I can see the way things are going. I can't help it. You'll see for yourself to-morrow. There'll be a full account of the inquest in the local papers. I saw two reporters scribbling away, damn them."

"The inquest," she faltered. "It's over then."

"No. Only just begun. They took formal evidence of identification and Cardew's evidence, and adjourned."

"Oh, don't they know what she died of?"

"They aren't satisfied," he said. "The police are enquiring into it."

"The police! Oh, Mark!"

"Yes. Both the maids attended the inquest. I suppose they'll be called next time. We had a taxi there and back. The police had it ready for us at the back of the Town Hall to avoid the crowd that had collected, and when we got home we found Gladys and the cook had had their boxes fetched in our absence. Fortunately there's a dear old woman who was with us years ago, first as a nurse-maid for Claire and me and afterwards as cook, and she had come in to look after George while we were all out. She's coming in to help for the present."

"But—" She was puzzled, conscious of something unexplained. "She—she didn't kill herself, did she?"

"Bertha? Why should she? No. She was happy enough," he said bitterly; "she enjoyed keeping us all under her thumb. She took after my father. He was like that, 'Do this!' and you did it, or there was a hell of a row"—he broke off to listen to the striking of the Town Hall clock. "Eleven. Ought you to go back, darling?"

"Another ten minutes," she murmured.

"All right."

They were silent now. After a while she made a tiny movement, and he released her with a sigh. "Thank you for coming, Lucy."

"I'll try to slip out again Saturday night."

"No, dear. This is the last time."

He heard her gasp. "Oh—why?"

"It's not fair to you. I'm not fit. It's got to end now."

"But I thought—" she faltered. "I'm ready to wait, Mark. I mean it."

Her cheeks burned in the darkness. Had she no pride? Was this what they meant when they said girls made themselves cheap?

"Perhaps you're trying to tell me that you don't really love me. You've just been amusing yourself?"

"Oh, God!" his voice was rough with pain. "I should never have let you do this. If people knew. If I thought I'd harmed you I'd shoot myself. Go home now, Lucy, and forget me."

"A quarter to twelve," said Miss Rivers as she switched on the light in the hall. "Not so bad. I told Mrs. Miller we wanted to get away early. I didn't quite like leaving the child in bed with her cold."

"It isn't serious, is it?" said the Colonel, unwinding his muffler. "Nothing more than a chill?"

"Just a chill," said his sister cheerfully. She was in good spirits for she had held excellent cards all the evening and had won four shillings and ninepence. "I'll just run up and make sure she's all right and then come down again for my cup of malted milk. Will you have malted milk, dear?"

"Whisky for me, thanks."

The Colonel went into the dining-room, turned on the gas fire, and mixed himself a whisky and soda. He, too, was in a contented mood. He had been lucky at his table; he was feeling uncommonly fit; those shares he had been worrying about had turned out better than he had dared to hope, and he was looking forward to a visit from his brother-in-law, Geoffrey Raynham. Geoff was a good fellow, interesting, too, for he had travelled a lot.

Miss Rivers came in with the milk she had been warming up on the gas ring in the kitchen. "The child is fast asleep," she announced.

"Good," said Lucy's father placidly. "I haven't told her about that letter I had from Raynham this morning. I'm glad he's coming down. He'll liven us up a bit. Sometimes I wonder if the life we lead isn't rather quiet for a young girl, eh?"

Miss Rivers repelled this suggestion vigorously. "Nonsense. Lucy is healthy but she isn't what I should call robust. The hectic existence of these bright young things one reads about would kill her. And I'm sure she's perfectly satisfied with her simple, wholesome pleasures, tennis and—and so on. She isn't one of the modern restless sort, thank Heaven. Good night, John."

"Good night, Mary."

CHAPTER VII

UNCLE AND NIECE

THE MILLERS dined at Simla on the evening of Geoffrey Raynham's arrival. Mrs. Miller, who sat between him and her host, found him pleasant but non-committal. He had travelled, she gathered, in the East. Tea planting? Well, not exactly. She hoped he would not find Dennyford too boring. They were proud of their links, and if he played bridge? He didn't? Mrs. Miller abruptly lost interest in him and turned to her host.

Geoffrey Raynham applied himself to his dinner. The dining-room blinds had not been drawn. He could see beyond the hedge of tamarisks the road and narrow strip of common, and beyond that the parade, raised like a dyke and dark against the last glimmer of light on the horizon. He fixed his monocle more firmly in his eye. While he talked to Mrs. Miller he had looked at his niece, whom he had last seen as a long-legged child of eight. Very charming in that pink frock, he thought. But why hadn't they asked some cheery boy to pair off with her? She must be bored among so many old fogies. Dear little Lucy.

He smiled at her and her answering smile reminded him rather poignantly of his dead sister.

Mr. Miller, who was, he had learned, the manager of the local branch of Barclay's Bank, was seated facing him on the right of their hostess. He spoke to him across the table.

"You are glad to be home?"

"For a while, yes. The atmosphere of a peaceful little place like this, so typically English, almost Jane Austen still in the twentieth century, where the most exciting thing that could happen would be the lowering of somebody's golf handicap, is very agreeable."

Miller laughed. "But you're wrong as it happens. Golf handicaps be blowed. If you've a taste for crime—"

Raynham's face changed slightly. One was not supposed to talk shop, especially if one's job was in the Far East.

"What sort of crime?" he asked idly.

"Murder."

The maid had set the dessert and left the room. "She's really managed very nicely!" thought Miss Rivers. Mrs. Miller, who had been telling the Colonel about her dahlias, broke off. There was one of those odd silences into which a general conversation drops as an aeroplane drops in an air pocket. Mrs. Miller broke it.

"Ned, you'd better tell them. Perhaps they haven't heard."

Mr. Miller cleared his throat. "Oh, well, it's just a rumour, but there's no smoke without fire, what? It's the Armour case. I heard this afternoon that a chemical analysis of the—er—remains has proved beyond a doubt that Bertha Armour died of arsenic poisoning, a dose, and a thundering big dose, administered a few hours before her death. Now, what do you say to that!"

"Terrible!" said the Colonel.

Miss Rivers was peeling a peach. She removed the kernel carefully.

"Dear me!" she murmured. "Who do they think did it?"

"I'm afraid it's fairly obvious," said Mr. Miller. Plainly he was enjoying himself. It was not often that he had hearers who hung on his words. His cherubic face registered a child-like disappointment when his host intervened.

"Sorry, Miller, but I think we'd better not discuss it. I'm on the Bench, you know, and I may have to go into the thing officially later on. Though I hope to Heaven," he added, "that there's some mistake."

Miss Rivers caught Mrs. Miller's eye. "And about time, too," thought Raynham. "What's the matter with Lucy?" He crossed the room to open the door for them and spoke to the girl as she passed out in the wake of the two older women. "I've got some Chinese embroideries for you and a jade necklace—my dear, are you ill?"

"How kind of you"—the sweet, husky voice faltered and steadied itself. "No. I'm quite all right."

Raynham looked after her thoughtfully. Poor Janet's baby. Motherless. No doubt her father and her aunt idolised her. He had seen that. But did they understand her? He closed the door and went back to the table. Miller was lighting a cigarette.

"Look here—I'm sorry if I was indiscreet just now," he said rather stiffly. It was apparent that he had resented the check.

The Colonel, who hated giving offence, looked red and uncomfortable. "You weren't, Miller. Not in the least. But, of course, in my position one has to be careful. One mustn't pre-judge a case, and this will be a fearful responsibility."

"The last word won't rest with you."

"No. That's one comfort."

"You don't know any of the family personally?" said Miller.

"No. They were here when we came. Miss Armour didn't call on newcomers, and the older residents didn't know them. Well, I needn't tell you that. One does not want to be censorious and Pharisaical, but they weren't the sort of people we're used to, and there was Lucy to consider. Shall we join the ladies?"

They found Miss Rivers and Mrs. Miller waiting with unconcealed impatience and the packs of cards laid out.

"You'll play in my stead to-night," the Colonel said to his brother-in-law. "You don't play? Is it possible? But what do you do with yourself?"

Raynham smiled. "I shall pass the time somehow. Where's Lucy?"

Miss Rivers answered. "She's gone to bed. She's got one of her headaches. The library books and this week's *Punch* are on that table. Do we cut for partners?"

Raynham took up a book but he did not read it. No one paid any further attention to him. He watched the players for a while with mingled irritation and amusement, noting Mrs. Miller's likeness to a highly respectable vulture and Mary Rivers' habit of rubbing her nose when in doubt. The women took their game more seriously than the men. Once, at least, the manager's wife lifted her voice in reproof and the Colonel apologised.

"Sorry! You're right. I must have been wool gathering."

At half-past ten Geoffrey Raynham, who had been suppressing yawns for some time, stood up. "I think I'll go to bed. Good night everybody."

They answered with perfunctory heartiness. "Good night."

"A hot bath!" he thought, but when he tried it the hot water tap ran cold. Of course, he told himself. He might have known Mary Rivers would be a bad housekeeper. Well, he need not stay over the week-end.

But later, much later, when the Millers had left and the house was quiet, he heard sounds coming from the room next his own that caused him to change his mind.

Lucy did not appear at breakfast the next morning. He heard that she was having it in bed, but hoped to come down later.

The Colonel suggested a round of golf.

"Not to-day, I think, thanks. I've some letters to write, and perhaps Lucy will be kind to her old uncle and take him for a walk later."

His brother-in-law acquiesced. Miss Rivers stated that she was going to be busy. She had to take the parish magazines round her district.

Raynham was alone in the dining-room when Lucy appeared. He jumped up, shook her passive hand and kissed her cold cheek.

"My dear. I'm afraid the head is still bad. Do you feel like a walk?"

"Not much."

"Will you come for a run in my car?"

"Have you got a car?"

"Didn't you know? I came down in it. But you were out when I arrived, weren't you. I bought it last week when I landed, and I shall sell it again when my leave is up. We'll make a day of it, shall we? Leave word we won't be back to lunch."

"Oh! very well."

Her manner, he felt sure, was not intentionally ungracious. It was as if she was only partly conscious of her surroundings. He saw that she was well wrapped up and then left her alone for a while. They had crossed the Downs and followed one of the winding by-roads that intersect the weald for some miles when he pulled up on a patch of common sheltered from the north by a copse of oak and hazel undergrowth.

"Lucy, when I came down I hoped you and I were going to be good pals."

"Yes, Uncle."

"Don't call me uncle. Call me Geoffrey."

"If you like."

"Lucy, I don't want to butt in, but I do want to help you if I can. I heard—I couldn't help hearing you crying in the night."

Silence. He watched the small gloved hands gripping the rug over her knees and was careful not to embarrass her further by lifting his eyes to her face. "Lucy," he said again very gently.

She answered with a great effort and in a voice that was barely audible, "Don't tell them—Daddy and Aunt Mary."

"All right. But you must trust me. I loved your mother, Lucy. If you'll tell me what the trouble is I'll try to put it right."

"Thank you. But there isn't anything you can do. Please. It's just—" She added something he could not catch. The only intelligible word was "unhappy." He waited, but no more came. He was sorry, but he could not be angry with her. After all, he was practically a stranger to her. He must be patient. But he had a feeling that time pressed.

"All right," he said. "Will you have a cigarette? No. You don't mind if I smoke?" He sat placidly contemplating the common patched with bracken turned to gold by the first frosts of October under the clear pale autumn sky. She was showing pluck, wasn't she, in trying to bear her burden, whatever it was, alone?

"All right," he said again as he rubbed out the stump of his cigarette in his ash tray before throwing it away. "But my offer holds. Come to me any time and I'll do my damndest. I'm staying on a few days. And don't be afraid of me," he added. "I shan't preach."

He laid his lean brown hand over hers for a moment before he took the steering wheel.

Chapter VIII

RAYNHAM'S FIRST MOVE

"Somebody to see me?" Superintendent Brisling read the name on the card. "Mr. Geoffrey Raynham."

"He's staying at Simla, sir, with Colonel Rivers. He passed me yesterday in his car when I was on point duty in the High Street. He had a young lady with him."

The young constable's tone was significant. Brisling nodded.

"Very good, Bennet. Show him in."

Brisling rose as his visitor entered. "Take a chair, Mr. Raynham." He resumed his seat at a littered writing table. "What can I do for you?"

Raynham did not answer immediately. He knew that the superintendent might resent his intervention in a case that did not concern him officially, and though he had a good reason for coming he was anxious to keep it to himself if possible. "Well—the fact is I'm in the police, too, Superintendent; another branch of the service."

Brisling's eyebrows went up. "Intelligence?"

"You've got it in one." Raynham mentioned a letter and a number and Brisling made a note of both on his pad.

"Just in case," he remarked. "No offence?"

"Of course not," said Raynham heartily. "Ring up Victoria 7000 now, if you like. But this visit isn't official. I'm on holiday. My job's abroad, east of Suez, and I'm home on leave. I'm staying here with my brother-in-law, Colonel Rivers, and I've been hearing a good deal of talk about the sudden death of a well known resident. I gathered that police enquiries were being made."

"Yes," said Brisling slowly. "We certainly are looking into the matter." He took up a pen and laid it down again.

There was a pause while the two men eyed each other.

Raynham leaned forward. "Look here," he said, "if you don't care to discuss it with me I'll get up and go. I've no earthly right here."

"I don't see everyone who asks for me," said Brisling. "Can you guess why you were shown in here, Mr. Raynham? It was because you are staying at Simla."

His visitor's face betrayed nothing. "Then I take it you are willing to talk things over? I need hardly say that your confidence will be respected. Do you mind if I smoke? Thanks. Try one of mine."

Brisling accepted a cigarette from Raynham's case. "As a matter of fact," he said, "I'd rather like to clear my mind by running over the points of the case. There's no doubt in my opinion that Miss Armour was murdered, and I'm pretty sure who did it. I expect to make an arrest before the inquest is resumed."

"Who is your suspect?"

"The victim's half-brother, Mark Armour." He waited a moment before he added, "Mind you, I hope to be able to keep Miss Lucy out of it."

Raynham started violently. "Lucy! Good God!"

Brisling looked at him. "I thought perhaps you knew that she was—interested—in young Armour. It's queer what a fascination a certain type of scoundrel has for women."

"You're sure he is a scoundrel? I mean—he has a bad reputation?"

"He forged his father's name to a cheque when he was a boy in his teens. I allow there were extenuating circumstances. Old Armour was a hard nut to crack. His second wife—the boy's mother—had run away with another man. The story is that she was down and out and wrote for help and that her son found her letter in the wastepaper basket and begged his father to do something for her. When the old man declined the boy got hold of his cheque book. Armour turned him out of the house. The War broke out a few weeks later and I believe he joined up. We don't know what he did after he was demobbed, but latterly he's been earning his living by preying on the vanity of elderly women, in a word, as a gigolo. He met with an accident in the summer that lamed him and he's been at home ever since, and champing his bit, no doubt. Old Armour left everything to his eldest daughter for her life. She was to provide her brothers and sisters with a home as long as they remained unmarried."

"And now the money will be divided?"

"Yes."

"What about the other brother and the sisters? Aren't they equally open to suspicion?"

"Hardly. The brother is half-witted, but, I gather, quite harmless. One of the sisters is odd. Peculiar in her dress and so forth. The younger sister is all right."

"There's a taint of insanity then?" said Raynham.

"Yes, but it won't help the defence to save their man from the drop," said the superintendent bluntly. "The first wife died in an asylum. It comes from her."

Raynham sighed. Lucy had not given him her confidence. He had guessed at some connection between her evident distress and the Armour case, hoping against hope that he was wrong. But the poor child's secret was evidently known to the police and if he was to be of any use to her he had better know it too.

He cleared his throat. "About my niece—"

"Ah!" said Brisling, "your coming like this, Mr. Raynham, takes a weight off my mind. That young lady's in need of a friend. Her father and her aunt think no end of her, I believe, and rightly, for a nicer young lady never stepped—but in their eyes she's just a child. That's their mistake. Children grow up into men and women, worse luck. She's been meeting young Armour on the beach at night."

"Good Lord!"

"Don't take it too hard, Mr. Raynham. Armour's a bad egg, but I think in this case—what I mean to say is the young lady has been foolish but I shouldn't think any—any irreparable damage has been done."

"She won't be dragged into this, Brisling."

"I hope not, but I can't make any promises," said the superintendent gravely. "You see—he couldn't marry while his sister lived. Now he'll have a fourth share of the estate. And—" he hesitated. "They were together up to midnight the night the murder was committed. She was seen to leave Simla and cross the common to the last shelter on the parade by the constable on the beat and he saw her going home again an hour later."

Raynham's lean, sunburned face was a mask concealing his anger and dismay. Lucy creeping out after dark to meet a lover, deceiving her father and her aunt, making herself cheap. Lucy. His sister's girl. The little fool. She ought to be whipped, he thought. And then, as he recalled her dumb despair, his heart was wrung with pity.

Aloud he said, "Isn't that a point in his favour? It's a case of poisoning by arsenic, isn't it? He was out all the evening. The poison may have been administered during his absence."

"If the defence makes that point they'll have to call Miss Rivers to prove where he was," said Brisling.

Raynham groaned. "It looks like the devil of a mess. And I suppose that kind of fellow won't think twice about sheltering himself at a girl's expense? I mean—we can't expect him to shield her when he's trying to save his neck? It would be rather much to ask even of a normally decent young man."

Brisling shook his head. "It cuts both ways. A love affair in which both parties, presumably, were looking forward to marriage supplies a motive for the crime."

"But, look here, you're not relying on that alone."

"He called on a young doctor down the road earlier in the evening. The doctor had been called out to attend a servant girl who had cut her hand. He found Armour waiting in his surgery when he returned. He explained that he had been unable to make anyone hear and had walked in. The doctor does his own dispensing and keeps his drugs in the room adjoining his surgery. I shouldn't tell everybody this, Mr. Raynham. I'm not sure that I ought to be telling you."

"I appreciate your confidence," said Raynham.

Brisling looked at his watch. "I'm afraid I haven't any more time just now."

Raynham, taking the hint, stood up. "I'm greatly obliged to you, Superintendent. You don't think of making an arrest for another day or two, I take it?"

"I do not. I'm having him watched, naturally. He can't possibly get away. I'm sure—but I'd like to be just a little surer before I burn my boats," confessed Brisling.

"I wonder if you'd object to my poking about a little on my own?"

Brisling frowned. Obviously he did not welcome the idea. But he was a kind-hearted man. "It's on your niece's account, I suppose. She'll be well rid of him."

"I daresay," said the other bitterly, "but I'm afraid that if I can't convince her that I'm doing all I can for him she may screw up her courage to appeal to you. It's the sort of thing a girl would think of. You don't want her crying her eyes out here, I imagine."

"Good Heavens, no!" The superintendent did not conceal his alarm at the prospect. "Don't let her do that, Mr. Raynham. Tell her it wouldn't be any good. I've got my duty." He wiped his brow. "You made me go hot all over. All right, Mr. Raynham. It's not as if you were one of these blundering amateurs. I don't mind—but what do you want to get at?"

"The truth."

"What a hope," murmured the superintendent with his wry smile. "Well, I've got a man in London looking into Armour's record there; the kind of people he was mixed up with and so forth, and when I've got his report my case will be virtually complete."

"Have you got Armour's statement."

"A short one. He left out a lot and we didn't press him. We'll have to put him through it again before we move. You can go ahead on your own lines if you want to, Mr. Raynham, but I must make one stipulation."

"What is it?"

"That you come straight to me with anything you may find."

Raynham recoiled. "I'm not going to help you to hang the man."

"Why not," said Brisling harshly, "if he's guilty?"

Raynham shuddered. He was thinking of Lucy. But Brisling was right. "Very well," he said. "I accept."

The superintendent nodded. "Come and see me again in any case," he said cordially. They shook hands. Raynham left the police station and walked back to his brother-in-law's house. The luncheon gong sounded as he entered the hall.

Colonel Rivers, who was already in the dining-room, called to him gaily.

"Where on earth have you been? I thought you'd be coming with me. I don't want you to get the idea that this place is dull. We're a happy little community, eh, Mary? I often say if I had to move I don't know where I'd go. Where's Lucy? Another headache? Mary, if this keeps on I think we shall have to take her to an oculist. It may be eye strain."

Chapter IX
BEDROCK

Lucy sat up in bed. "Who is it?"

"It's me. Geoffrey. May I come in, Lucy? I want to talk to you and this is a good opportunity. Your father and aunt have gone to one of their bridge parties. I was invited, but I got out of it. The maid's gone home, and we're alone in the house. Put on your dressing-gown and come down if you'd rather. There's a good fire in the morning-room."

"All right," she called back. "I'll be down in five minutes."

He was sitting by the fire, smoking, when she came slowly into the room. He looked up and was touched by her pallor and the dark rings round her eyes.

"Sit here, my dear. Will you have another cushion? How's your head?"

"I can bear it. What did you want to say to me?"

"Lucy, I know everything."

He heard her gasp and saw her hands grip the arms of her chair.

"I want to help you," he said quickly.

"How did you—f-find out?"

"Never mind that now." He could not harden his heart enough to tell her crudely that her stolen meetings with her lover had been noted by the local police.

"You won't tell Daddy. He's so—he wouldn't understand. He'd be so frightfully shocked."

"I think he would," Raynham agreed. His tone was grave. "I'm not pleased with you, Lucy. But I haven't brought you down here to scold you. If I could arrange for an old friend of mine in India to ask you to go out to her for the winter, would you go? She's a charming woman and kindness itself and she enjoys giving girls a good time. She's no daughters of her own."

"No."

"Think, Lucy. You can do no good here, and if other people get to know what I know it may come round to your father and cause him a great deal of pain."

"I can't go."

Raynham's face hardened. "I see I shall have to speak more plainly. The police have evidence that Miss Armour was murdered. They are making enquiries, and sooner or later there will be an arrest and a trial with all the ghastly publicity that involves. If we are not very careful you may be drawn into this case, called upon to answer questions in the witness-box. I'm not thinking of you only, though I'd give a good deal to save you from such an ordeal. I'm thinking of your father, well known and respected here, happy in his ignorance—" he stopped, afraid of saying too much.

"I'm sorry," she said faintly.

"Then you'll be a sensible girl and go while the going's good. Leave all the arrangements to me. You've only got to acquiesce."

She shook her head. "You said you knew everything. I see you don't. If you did you would understand that I can't possibly go away and leave Mark in such trouble. I love him. I love him terribly."

The naked sincerity of that utterance silenced Raynham for a moment though he had been half prepared for it. It made everything more difficult. And yet he knew that if she had grasped at his offer he would have been vaguely disappointed. He was idealist enough to be relieved that she had not slipped out of the house after dark "just for fun."

"My dear," he said more gently, "you won't help by staying here. If he cares for you your going away for a time will probably be a weight off his mind."

"Why?"

"He can't want you to be mixed up in this business."

"I don't see why I should be mixed up in it," she said. "I don't know his family at all. I've never been to the house."

"You were with him down on the Front the night his sister died," said Raynham.

Lucy's cheeks burned. "Yes, I was," she said defiantly, "and I'll meet him again whenever he asks me."

"Has he asked you lately?"

"Only once since—since that happened. To say good-bye."

Raynham glanced at the clock. She must get back to her room before her father and aunt returned from their bridge party.

"Now listen to me, Lucy," he said, "I offered to help you yesterday when I didn't know what was wrong. That offer still holds. You must give up any idea you ever had of marrying this young man. That's quite impossible. You tell me he's said good-bye. That shows that he realises himself that he isn't fit for you. Now you're very young, my dear, and inexperienced, and you've got romantic ideas from the poetry and novels you've read. You may even have some scheme of offering yourself to him or persuading him to run away with you or some nonsense of that sort. I know I sound brutal, but I want you to understand the position. The police suspect him of poisoning his sister. He couldn't marry while she lived as he was entirely dependent on her. Now he gets a fourth share of the estate. His affair with you supplies a motive for the crime. Now do you see why you must leave him alone?"

He watched the colour fade from her face, leaving her white to the lips.

"Alone," she whispered. "Oh, Mark!" Tears were running down her cheeks. She fumbled blindly for a handkerchief. Raynham passed her his. Poor child, he thought. Well, they had got down to bedrock at last.

"Uncle Geoffrey."

"Yes, Lucy."

"He didn't do it. He couldn't. Not poison. He has no friends here. He's never had a chance. He's always been unhappy. Can't you help him?"

"If I undertake to try," he said, "will you promise not to do anything without first consulting me?"

"Yes."

"Just go on quietly as usual."

"What will you do?"

"I shall go back to Town to-morrow morning and come back in the afternoon, but not to Simla. I must approach the case from a new angle."

"Shall I hear from you?" she asked wistfully.

"Yes. But you must not be impatient. You must trust me," he hesitated. "I'll tell you a secret, Lucy. You've been a bit vague about my job in the East, haven't you? Something in the Civil Service, eh? Well, that's near enough for the general public, but it's a branch of the Intelligence. In short, a kind of sleuth. I've had a good bit of experience one way and another, so there is a chance I may find out a bit more than the local bobbies. And now run back to bed. Be brave, Lucy. Good night, my dear."

Chapter X

MRS. TRANT'S LODGERS

The two cottages stood back from the road in a patch of garden. They were flint walled and thatched and had been standing there before the branch line to Dennyford had been made. Now one of them was occupied by a signalman and his wife and the other by Bessie Trant. Bessie had been in service at the White House before she married Trant. Since his death she had let two of her rooms. One of them was let to the Armours' gardener and the other was vacant.

"Of course," said Bessie. "I 'ad the bill in the window and clean forgot to take it down. I don't know, I'm sure." She eyed the rather shabby, elderly man standing on her doorstep doubtfully. His dusty shoes were trodden over. He looked tired, and she noticed that he sighed as he bent to pick up his battered suit-case.

"Wait a bit," she said, "it's like this, you see. The maids up at White House went off the day of the funeral. Girls are like that nowadays. No consideration. And I'm going up there daily to oblige and only too glad to, Master Mark and Miss Claire being my own children in a manner of speaking. So if I took you in you'd have to make do the same as my other lodger with cold boiled bacon and tinned stuff while I'm so put about. Would it be for long?"

"A few days. I'm a canvasser. I'd be willing to pay in advance. My name's Roberts," said Raynham.

"Well—step in and I'll show you the room."

He followed her up the ladder-like stairs. The room was small and so low pitched that he could only stand upright at one end. He observed with satisfaction that it was very clean, but he had meant to take it in any case. He produced a grimy pound note, but Mrs. Trant waved it away.

"I don't want that. I can read faces. You won't bilk me. Tea'll be ready in half an hour when Lee comes in from his work. He's gardener up at White House and he's doing a bit extra carrying coals and boot cleaning to help me out. Come down to the kitchen when you're ready. You'll find a bit of soap and a towel in the scullery if you want a wash."

Raynham sat down on the end of the bed and filled and lit his pipe. He had heard of Mrs. Trant from a porter at the station of whom he had enquired for lodgings. The porter had told him of others.

"But you'll find Mrs. Trant a good sort though she is mixed up with those Armours. You've read about them in the paper I daresay."

Raynham felt he had made an excellent beginning. Obviously Mrs. Trant was a great talker. With a little encouragement she would impart all the information he required. Raynham waited until he heard his fellow lodger pumping water and talking to his landlady in a slow deep voice, and then went down. He found Mrs. Trant dishing up a liberal supply of fried bacon and eggs.

"There you are," she said heartily. "This is Mr. Roberts, Dick."

"Good evening," said Raynham.

The young man mumbled something in answer. He was evidently very shy. Raynham noticed the breadth of his shoulders and the way his brown hair curled on the nape of his neck. He needed a shave and there was earth under his nails, but he could not be described as either rough or dirty. There was something friendly about him. He was like a horse that comes trotting along a hedge and stands gazing at you over the gate as you pass. Clearly his landlady was fond of him. She heaped his plate with food.

"You eat all that. You need it, a chap of your size. He could make his fortune as a boxer with a bit of training, Mr. Roberts, but he 'asn't got the fighting spirit. Too soft and kind like. Wouldn't hurt a fly, would you, Richard Lee."

"I can't say that," rumbled Lee. "I've done for a good many in my time. Likewise wasps. And slugs."

"Lee's gardener up at White House," explained Mrs. Trant. "Did you finish clipping the hedge, Dick?"

"I'll finish he to-morrow. Miss Claire wanted me to see about the bulbs."

"So that was it. I saw 'er talking to you down by the potting shed."

Lee turned very red and said nothing more. Raynham asked for a second cup of tea. During the few hours he had spent in London he had supervised the printing of the leaflets he had brought with him for distribution, and had paid a flying visit to Scotland Yard. There had been no time for lunch. After the meal Mrs. Trant cleared away and sat down by the fire with a basket of mending, and the two men lit their pipes. Raynham discovered that his landlady was ready and even anxious to discuss the tragedy at the White House.

"Miss Bertha was no favourite of mine. We had words years ago when the second Mrs. Armour ran away. I'd have stayed on for the sake of Master Mark and Miss Claire, but I got a month's notice and I hadn't been inside the house since, not until the day of the funeral, when Miss Claire came round herself to ask me if I would. And I said to her then—'Is it true that there was arsenic found at the bottom of the glass of milk Miss Bertha had on her bedside table?' For I'd heard talk, you see, with the maids leaving like that and telling folks they were afraid to stay with a poisoner loose about the house."

"And what did she say?" enquired Raynham as the good woman paused for breath.

"She looked at me with those big dark eyes of hers and she said, 'Oh, nannie, I can't believe it. Unless she took something accidentally. She did take things for indigestion sometimes."

"That doesn't seem very likely," said Raynham.

"That's what I thought," Mrs. Trant confessed, "and I've lain awake wondering. If there was arsenic in that glass somebody must have put it there, somebody in the house. You've got six to choose from. The cook and the housemaid, Master George—but he hasn't the sense to do such a thing—Miss Winnie, and my two. Well, Miss Bertha talked very sharp to the servants and kept a sharp eye on the store cupboard. Why shouldn't that cook have been one of the kind that turns nasty when spoken to? 'Twas she carried up the glass of milk from the pantry every night. If I was the police I'd lay that cook by the 'eels and leave my betters alone."

"What I say is," mumbled Lee, "the less said the better."

"That's right." Mrs. Trant, like most ardent conversationalists, was impervious to hints, and the spate of words flowed on unchecked. "There's been a deal too much talk about those poor things from first to last. As if it was the children's fault that their mother ran away. It was the old man drove her to it, with his fault finding, and Miss Bertha took after him. Nag, nag, nag, all day long. They'll be happier now, I daresay, when this fuss and bother's over. Master George is as quiet as a lamb, and though Miss Winnie's a trial at times she's not bad tempered."

Lee knocked out the ashes of his pipe. "I'm going out for a bit."

"It's raining."

"Rain don't hurt."

He went into the scullery. They heard the sound of vigorous ablutions. Mrs. Trant chuckled as she drew a much mended sock over her hand and started on a gaping hole.

"Going to meet your young lady, Dick?"

"No." Raynham thought he sounded angry. "I believe I left the door of the greenhouse open. I'm going up to see. There might be a ground frost if the rain stops."

The door banged.

"I tease him a bit," said the old woman. There was mischief in her wrinkled face.

"So I see," said Raynham, smiling. "Has he got a young lady?"

"He may have," she said, "he's out most nights. But I don't know. He's one of the quiet sort. Terrible shy with girls. I had a niece of mine here once, a saucy little piece, and she couldn't get a word out of him."

Raynham got up. He was tired after a long day and disliked leaving the fireside, but he had to keep his word to Lucy. He had promised her to do his best. "I think I'll go for a turn," he said, forestalling her protests. "I can't sleep if I don't get a breath of fresh air the last thing."

The night was black as pitch, with a fine rain falling. He had trudged up the road from the town at dusk and had taken his bearings then. The railway bridge was a hundred yards further on. As he walked towards it there was a rumble and a roar as the last train from Dennyford to the junction passed through the cutting. He crossed the bridge. There were fields on his right, and on the left, screened from the highway by a high stone wall and a dense mass of trees and shrubberies, the house in which, only a few days earlier, a woman had been done to death.

As his eyes grew accustomed to the darkness he was able to discern the white painted gate.

He approached it cautiously and stood listening, prepared to hear the young gardener's footsteps on the gravel of the drive. It could not take him long to close the greenhouse door if that was really all he had come for. He waited, and after a while his patience was rewarded. He heard the footsteps of two people. Instinctively he moved back, standing close against the wall. They seemed to have stopped before they reached the gate but so close to it that he could hear their hurried breathing. There was a silence followed by some whispering. Then Lee said huskily, "D'you think I don't feel it just as much? But we got to be careful. We've got to wait."

The voice that answered was a woman's. "I'm sick of waiting."

There was another pause before the gate was unlatched. Lee came out, passing Raynham so close that the latter could have put out his hand and touched him, and walked back over the bridge.

CHAPTER XI

NOCTURNE

MRS. TRANT brought her new lodger an early cup of tea and informed him that his breakfast was laid and the kettle on the oil stove.

"Lee's gone to his work and I'm just off," she added.

"I'll be back between four and five. They've only me to depend on, you see. Go out by the back door, please, Mr. Roberts, and lock it and hide the key under the middle flower-pot on the window sill of the scullery. That's where I always put it."

Raynham got into his clothes. He missed his bath, but a morning tub was not in his part, and he had found a rigid attention to small details essential to success when he assumed any form of disguise. It was one of his axioms that the olfactory sense plays a greater part in life than is generally recognised. He relied as little as possible on the more obvious forms of make up, grease paint or false hair, though in the East it had sometimes been necessary to stain his skin. To go unwashed and unshaven, to slouch his shoulders and drag his feet, and alter the timbre and intonation of his voice, was generally sufficient, and he thought it would be so in this case, especially as he was a stranger in Dennyford.

He ate a hearty breakfast and smoked a pipe afterwards.

Among the china dogs and shell ornaments on the kitchen mantelpiece he had noticed a photograph of two children in a faded plush frame. He looked at it more closely. Written in one corner in a round childish hand he saw the names, Mark and Claire, with our love to dear Nannie. The little boy was holding his sister's hand. They were a charming pair. There was something touching about their innocent gravity. Obviously they had been beautiful children. Raynham did not wonder that even now their old nurse would not hear a word in disparagement of "my two."

Raynham sighed as he replaced the photograph. "Whom the gods love," he thought. How much better for everyone if the boy whose big dark eyes seemed to follow him about the room had died in childhood.

He left the cottage, hiding the door key as directed, and made his way into the town. In his role of door to door canvasser he was hoping to interview the two maids who had been at White House when Bertha Armour died. The superintendent had supplied him with their names and addresses.

"They've been warned not to chatter," he had said with his grim smile, "but I daresay you'll be able to get something out of them." Raynham hoped so, though he realised that his unshaven and dishevelled appearance would go against him. In the case of Gladys Pierce fortune favoured him, for she answered the door herself, and though she accepted the leaflet he pressed upon her reluctantly she stopped to listen and thawed perceptibly when he followed it up with the gift of a tin of shoe polish.

"This is the stuff, Miss. We're not giving free samples, not to everyone. It's left to our discretion. It's got to be somebody, if you'll excuse me saying so, with a neat, pretty foot that's likely to come in for favourable notice, and be a good walking advertisement. We'd like when your friends say, 'Your shoes always look so nice, dear!' for you to answer, 'I always use Gleamo.' There. It's a large size tin, you see. It would cost you a shilling in a shop."

"Well, I'm much obliged, I'm sure," said Miss Pierce graciously. "I don't mind trying it."

A friendly chat followed and Miss Pierce was led to refer to the death of her last employer.

"Horrible, it was," she said with an unaffected shudder. "I wake up nights even now fancying I hear her groaning. It was like seeing someone on one of those racks they tell about. She was a strong woman and she fought for her life. Suffer! I hope I never see anyone suffer like that again. I'll tell you towards the last I was praying, 'God, let her die! Let her die!' though she was quiet after the nurse came. And afterwards when Miss Watts—that's the cook—and I talked it over and understood that she'd been given a dose of rat poison we fair got the jim-jams. Because it stands to reason whoever did it was in the house, and what was there to stop them from trying again? I never had cared about living with a pair of loonies about, but they'd both seemed harmless enough. Still, as cook says, you never can tell. So we packed our boxes while the family was at the funeral and skedaddled."

"A pair of loonies!" exclaimed her interlocutor. "That's right. Mr. George is one. He was next in age to Miss Bertha. He spends his time cutting pictures out of papers and pasting them in albums when he isn't digging in his bit of garden. Just a softy I always thought. Timid and shy. Miss Claire can manage him best. I don't believe he's got it in him to do such a thing, but on the other hand I saw him fire up once when Miss Bertha was bullying her sister. He'd looked frightened for a bit, and then suddenly he turned quite red and he said, 'If you make Claire cry I'll kill you!' Miss Bertha was startled I can tell you. She didn't say another word."

"When was this?"

"Oh, some time ago. In the spring. Miss Claire quieted him and he never broke out again to my knowledge."

"You said a pair," he prompted her.

She laughed. "That's right. Miss Winnie. Man mad, poor thing. But there again it's just silliness, hanging round after a clergyman or something, and leaving bunches of flowers on the doorstep. Well, I mustn't stop here talking."

Raynham took the hint. He was going to see the cook, but he put leaflets in every door down that road first. His friend at Scotland Yard, Inspector Collier, sometimes chaffed him about his thoroughness, maintaining that if he played Othello he would black himself all over.

The cook was staying with a married sister who kept a lodging house on the Marine Parade and she answered the door, but she was older than Gladys Pierce and more on her guard, and though she accepted the proffered tin of shoe polish she declined to be drawn into conversation and shut the door in his face.

"And that's that!" he thought as he trudged away. He got a glass of beer and a ham sandwich for his lunch at a public house and spent the afternoon sitting on the beach smoking his pipe and watching the tide coming in. He was going to call on Doctor Cardew in the character of an out-patient and had to wait for his surgery hours. Meanwhile he tried to dismiss the case from his mind and to let his brain lie fallow. At six he got up, leaving the gulls crying in the gathering dusk over the deserted sand dunes, and turned inland.

After the brightly lit High Street the road that led through fields past the gas works and the allotments to the railway bridge seemed dark and dreary. The row of tall stuccoed houses standing solitary and aloof on the left loomed dark against the lingering glow of a stormy sunset. As Raynham approached the flight of steps leading up to the door of number one he noticed a woman standing by the railings.

He rang the bell and waited. After a moment some instinct made him look up. He received a shock at seeing a man's face peering down at him through the fanlight over the door. The face vanished and the door was opened just wide enough to allow him to pass in. The young man who had admitted him shut it again and turned the key.

"Sorry," he said. "I hope I didn't startle you just now."

"As a matter of fact you did," said Raynham.

"I had to see who it was," exclaimed Cardew. "I'm living in a state of siege. Are you a patient? Come in"—he led the way from the bare gas-lit hall into the surgery.

"I can't stand much more of it," he complained. "I shall be ruined if this goes on." He was too exasperated to care what the effect of his words might be on his visitor. He reminded Raynham of an over-driven horse, his eyes glaring, his muscles twitching.

"Sit down," he said, but he walked about the room himself, unable to keep still for a moment or concentrate his attention on his visitor.

Raynham waited, and as he waited he willed the other to be quiet. He was no hypnotist, but he had a very definite personality and could, when he chose, exert a calming influence. Cardew passed his big freckled fingers through his mop of sandy hair and sighed heavily. Then he tried, with some measure of success, to resume his professional manner. "Now—what can I do for you?"

Raynham explained that he had been troubled about his heart.

"I'll sound you. Just take off your coat and waistcoat. Oh Lord!" The front door bell rang, followed by a sub-dued but prolonged knocking. "There she is again. Was there a woman outside?"

"Yes. Standing by the railings."

The doctor ground his teeth. "How can I sound you while that row's going on! Thank God, my housekeeper's stone deaf. Come on. I'll do my best."

He adjusted the stethoscope and went about the busi-ness grimly with set lips. Presently he looked up. "Nothing wrong that I can make out. Of course after fifty we've all got to be careful. That will be half a crown. You're not on the panel? Right. I'll let you out. If that woman's there be careful she doesn't slip past you. I won't have her in here."

"If she's annoying you why don't you ring up the police?"

"I can't do that. I should feel such a fool. I—I—a man's helpless in such a position. No one who hasn't experi-enced it can imagine how damnable it is. She goes home for her meals. All the rest of the day she's either mooning about outside or ringing my bell, dropping notes or push-ing flowers through the letter box. And I've been working up a practice. I was beginning to get on. I say—don't talk about this, will you?"

"I won't."

They were in the hall now. Cardew moved the chair by the umbrella stand. "I'll just look through the fanlight before I open the door for you," he whispered. He climbed on the chair and peered out.

Raynham felt no inclination to smile. "Well?" he said.

"She's sitting on the kerb. She's crying. Man, this can't go on! Will you do something for me?"

"If I can."

"You're a stranger in the place, aren't you?"

"Yes."

"Turn to the left when you get out and go a quarter of a mile down the road and over the railway bridge. There's a largish house on the other side of the line, standing in its own grounds. You can't miss it. Ask for Mr. Armour. Tell him he must come and fetch his sister home and keep her away from me or I can't be responsible for anything I may do. No! Don't repeat that last bit. Just ask him to fetch her. He'll understand. Look here"—Cardew felt in his pockets—"have that half-crown back again for your trouble."

He had been too worried to pay much attention to his visitor, but he had got a general impression of down-at-heel shabbiness. Raynham, rather reluctantly, accepted the coin. He might awaken suspicion if he declined it. "That's all right, doctor," he said. "I'll tell him. Open the door now. She's not looking this way."

He heard the key turned in the lock as he went down the steps. Cardew was taking no chances. The woman, hearing him, glanced round quickly and stumbled to her feet, mumbling as he passed her something about a stone in her shoes and waiting for a friend.

"Poor thing," he thought, "she's ashamed of herself."

He remembered what Gladys Pierce had said about Winifred Armour, and the hints of the superintendent. He pitied her, but he pitied her victims even more. He knew what that kind of persecution might mean to a young man like Cardew. Probably, he thought, her pursuit of her quarry had intensified since her sister's death. He had gathered that Miss Armour had been a restraining influence. How long had Winifred been haunting the young doctor's house? Raynham recalled the glimpse he had had through a half open door of the dispensary behind the surgery. Jars and bottles on the shelves. But to choose the right one would need some elementary knowledge of chemistry. No theories yet, he admonished himself. Go on collecting impressions. He was about to see the other members of the Armour family under circumstances that might lead to some interesting revelations of character.

It was too dark to see the house when he reached it. There were lights in several windows and somebody was playing the piano. He rang the bell and the music ceased abruptly. There was rather a long interval before the door was opened by a young man.

"Mr. Mark Armour?"

"Yes. What do you want?"

"May I come in for a moment? I have a message for you from Doctor Cardew."

"Come in."

Mark led the way into the dining-room. A fire was burning on the hearth and the table was laid for supper. He turned up the gas.

"Now?" he said.

Raynham looked at that beautiful dusky face and his heart sank. Poor Lucy! No wonder she had succumbed. Any woman would. Beautiful—and worthless. Though— he tried to be fair—it was not a bad or even a weak face. There was no betraying slackness in the fine lines of the mouth and chin, and the brown eyes, though they looked weary and bloodshot, met his steadily.

"Well—what's the message?"

"Your sister is there, Mr. Armour. He'd be glad if you'd fetch her away. She's been there all day, waiting about outside his house. She only comes home to meals. He says he can't stand it."

"Poor devil!" said Mark. "I don't blame him. So that's where she's been. Who are you?"

"I'm a stranger here. I happened to be at the surgery. It's his time for seeing out-patients," explained Raynham.

"I see." Mark shrugged his shoulders. "All our troubles are public property. Just a minute"—he went to the door and called, "Claire!"

Claire came into the room with a quick glance at the stranger. Her brother repeated the substance of Cardew's message. "Poor thing," she said. "But—oh, I wish she wouldn't."

Mark sighed. "No use talking to Winnie. I'll fetch her home. We're fated to be a public spectacle."

Raynham followed him out of the house and caught him up before he reached the gate. "I'm coming your way."

"Are you? What was she doing when you left her?"

"Sitting on the kerb crying."

"Oh Lord! In the middle of a jeering crowd?"

"No, no, not as bad as that. It's a quiet road and dark. There wasn't anyone about."

"Thank God for that." After a moment he added, "Decent of you to come for me."

They crossed the bridge and reached the terrace of gaunt Victorian houses looming dark against the flat, misty background of fields.

"It's queer," said Mark, half to himself, "I always had a horror of these houses. I used to have nightmares about them when I was a small boy, horrid dreams of black beetles swarming up the area steps and through the railings and pursuing me down the road."

As they walked along the pavement a shadow detached itself from the railings of number one and moved towards them.

"Is that you, Winnie?"

Mark spoke gently. Raynham thought him remarkably long suffering.

"Oh, Mark." Winnie blew her nose and made a pathetic effort to appear normal—"Are you going to call on the doctor? Because, if so, I might go in with you just for a minute. I—I happened to be passing."

"Not to-night, Winnie. He's tired, and it's past his time for seeing patients. Come home with me."

"How do you know he's tired?" she said sharply.

"I judge him by myself, Winnie, I'm dead to the world."

"I don't know why you should be. You've nothing to do."

"Perhaps that's why," he said drearily. "Come along, my dear." He took her arm, but she hung back.

"Don't hustle me. He needs a wife, Mark. Someone to look after him and love him."

"Come along."

"I ought to give him a chance to thank me for the flowers I brought him. I couldn't make anyone hear, and at last I pushed them through the letterbox."

"Another time. Come home with me now."

She began to cry again. "You're all against me. You're as bad as Bertha."

Raynham watched the two figures, the woman stumbling, the man supporting her with his arm, vanish into the darkness. Should he knock again at the doctor's door and reassure him? On the whole he thought not. He too was tired after a long day, and felt he had earned a cup of tea and a pipe and the pleasant warmth of Mrs. Trant's kitchen fire. He had learnt a good deal. It remained to be seen if any of the pieces he had picked up would fit into the puzzle he was trying to solve.

Chapter XII
THE ONLY QUESTION

Mark Armour was alone in the dining-room when Mrs. Trant, in a hissing whisper, announced that "that policeman" had called again.

Mark flinched a little. Was he never to be left in peace? "Which policeman, Nannie?"

"The superintendent. He's not in uniform. He says can he have a few words with you?"

"Of course. Show him in."

Mrs. Trant, with an air of mute protest, introduced Brisling, and left the two men together. Mark waved his unwelcome visitor to a chair and offered his cigarette case.

Brisling shook his head. "No, thank you, sir. I seldom smoke while on duty. But don't let me stop you from having one."

"Thanks. I've been smoking too much lately. Tobacco soothes the nerves, you know. How are you getting on with your enquiry, Superintendent?"

"Pretty well," said Brisling stolidly, "but I just wanted to check up a bit on the statement you made when I came here the other day. You needn't answer any questions, but, on the other hand, if you can assist us it would be all to the good, wouldn't it?"

"Naturally," Mark agreed.

"What I mean is, here you are, all of you, can't settle to anything or go away for a change, or make any arrangements until the inquest on your sister is over. Very unpleasant I'm sure," said the superintendent sympathetically.

"You'd think so if you had to live in this damned house," Mark replied.

"You don't care for the place?"

"I loathe it. Always did. It's dark and damp. Too many trees and shrubberies."

"You'll be selling it perhaps?"

"I hope so." He was interrupted by a muffled roar and the ornaments on the mantelpiece shook. Brisling half rose from his seat.

Mark laughed. "The 11.15 from the Junction. The line runs at the bottom of our garden. Had you forgotten that?"

"I had for the moment," Brisling acknowledged. "Well, I must not take up too much of your time."

"Don't worry about that," said Mark. "I have nothing whatever to do. I'm completely useless and superfluous. I say, Superintendent, if I'd been killed in the war would they have put my name with the others on the local memorial? I've often wondered."

"Of course," said Brisling.

"How nice of them!"

He sounded a shade too grateful, and Brisling looked at him sharply. Was young Armour pulling his leg? He was not going to stand any nonsense of that sort though he was willing to make allowances. He had seen men being trapped before. They were apt to hit out rather wildly as they became aware of the strangling meshes of the net as it was drawn closer and closer. He produced his notebook and turned over the pages.

"You went over to Brighton on the 23rd and had tea at the Metropole with a lady. You didn't mention her name, but we know it—Mrs. Lobb."

Mark bit his lip. How furious Violet Lobb would be if they dragged her into the case. Of course she had known that he hoped to borrow from her. Had she been fool enough to tell the police that? Aloud he said coolly, "Quite right. I used to be her dancing partner before I damaged my leg."

"We know that, Mr. Armour. On your way home you called on Doctor Cardew. Why was that?"

"It was an impulse. I thought I'd ask him whether I should get over my limp. I happened to be passing at the hour he saw out-patients."

"Did his housekeeper admit you?"

"No. I rang but nobody came so I turned the door-handle and walked in. The surgery door was open. I went in and waited until the doctor came. He'd been called out to attend a servant girl who cut herself."

"How long were you alone there in the surgery?"

"I don't know. Five minutes. It might have been more. Does it matter?"

"You dined at home with the rest of the family?"

"Yes."

"At what hour?"

"Between seven and eight."

"You went out again later?"

"Yes."

"Where did you go?"

"Oh, I just walked about."

"Were you alone?"

"Yes."

"You didn't meet anyone you knew?"

"No one."

"Rather an extraordinary way of spending the evening, wasn't it, Mr. Armour? A dark chilly autumn night. And you with a limp."

"I don't think so. I like walking at night."

"You came in late, after midnight?"

"Yes."

"The household had retired to rest?"

"Oh, yes."

"You had a latchkey?"

"No. Bertha—my sister wouldn't have stood for that. The others never went out at night."

"Then how did you obtain admittance? I didn't ask you this before, Mr. Armour, but the point occurred to me."

"By the french window in the little study. The latch is defective and can be lifted easily with the blade of a pocket knife. I used to slip in and out that way when I was a boy."

"I understand. Perhaps you'd let me see it presently."

"Certainly. My brother George uses that room during the day."

"You got in without disturbing anyone and went straight up to your bedroom? Is that correct?"

"Yes."

"Did you notice the time?"

"No."

"Was it after one o'clock?"

"I shouldn't think so."

"You went to bed directly?"

"I—yes."

He suppressed a nervous movement. Why did Brisling fix him with that unwinking stare? What was he getting at? He took a cigarette from his case and lit it. The superintendent leaned forward.

"How do you account for the fact that when the cook, fancying she heard somebody moving about on the floor below, peeped over the banisters, she saw you crossing the landing? You were fully dressed and it was then a quarter to three—"

"I'd been reading. I was tired but not sleepy."

"Why had you left your room?"

"The cook fancied she heard a noise below. So did I. I went out as she did to investigate."

"I see," said Brisling reflectively. "Did you make any discoveries?"

"None."

"What happened after that?"

"I undressed and got into bed."

"Didn't you get up again when your sister—I should say your half-sister—was taken ill?"

"I slept through a part of that. I had taken a couple of aspirin. Claire came in and roused me between six and seven and I got up at once, but there wasn't anything I could do."

"Thank you, Mr. Armour." Brisling stood up. "I'll have a look at that window now."

Mark led the way to the study where George, busy with his paste pot and scissors, looked shyly away from them and pretended not to hear the superintendent's good morning.

Brisling examined the defective window catch. "Quite easy," he said as he slipped in the blade of his clasp knife. "And you step out on a gravel path that leads round the back of the house to the drive, eh? What happens if you cross the lawn? Is there a back gate?"

"No."

"Were you the only member of the family who knew of this way out, Mr. Armour?"

"Claire knew, but I don't suppose she's used it since we were children. We used to slip out sometimes to watch the last train pass through the cutting and under the bridge, like a fire breathing dragon."

"I see," said Brisling smiling, "a pair of young imps. I may as well go out this way. Perhaps you'll walk down the drive with me. I'm sorry to have to keep barging in like this, Mr. Armour."

"It's your job," said Mark.

"Not a pleasant one," said the superintendent with feeling. "I'd like to think that you appreciate my difficulty. I haven't asked you for suggestions, Mr. Armour. I take it that if you could assist us to clear up the mystery of your sister's death you would do so."

Mark hesitated. "Isn't it possible that she committed suicide?"

Brisling shook his head. "The evidence of those who were with her during her last hours is against it. The doctor, the cook, the nurse who was fetched, your sister, Claire, all agree that she fought for her life. There was time and opportunity for her to admit that she had taken poison if she had taken it knowingly. No, Mr. Armour. The coroner's jury's verdict will certainly be murder, the only question is whether it will be against a person or persons unknown, or—"

They had reached the entrance gate. Brisling had left his bicycle leaning against a tree. He wheeled it out on to the road.

"Good morning," he said, and rode away. Mark, looking after him, reflected that he had not offered to shake hands.

Chapter XIII
GOOD ADVICE

The superintendent was in his office after lunch when Raynham called and was shown in. Brisling, rising to greet him, noticed that he was looking very spruce in a new grey suit, with a monocle screwed into his eye.

"Well!" he said, "have you come to throw up the sponge?"

"Certainly not."

"You've been making enquiries in London? I thought I told you we were doing that. You went up by road on Tuesday morning."

Raynham smiled. "And came back by train the same evening. I passed you in the High Street the next day, Superintendent, but you didn't know me."

"Your score," conceded Brisling. "Of course I had heard you were an adept at that sort of thing, though in this case it seems hardly necessary. Did you make any discoveries?"

"I saw and heard several of the people involved in this business when they were off their guard."

"And have you come to any conclusion?"

Raynham took a cigarette from his case and tapped it on the back of his hand. "I rather like young Armour," he said.

"The fellow is a professional charmer," Brisling reminded him.

"He may be. Don't let's judge him for that, Brisling," said the other man earnestly. "He's never had a dog's chance if all I hear is true. I'm prepared to admit that he's earned a sort of living cadging round and, if required, making love to silly old women. In short, a gigolo. But a man may sink as low as that and yet be utterly incapable of cold-blooded murder."

"In my experience," said Brisling, "anybody's capable of anything. I'm sorry, Mr. Raynham, but that psychological stuff cuts no ice with me. It wouldn't with you if you were in this officially. We have to go by the evidence."

"There were five other people in the house the night the murder was committed. Any one of them may be guilty. The cook who carried the glass of milk up to Miss Armour's room during dinner, the housemaid who went in afterwards to turn down the bed, the other brother, the two sisters."

There was a pause. Brisling was drawing noughts and crosses on his blotter. He looked up presently. His face was very grave. "I'll tell you something. We found a half finished tin of weed killer in the potting shed."

"Then any one of—"

"Wait! There's something else. The sediment in the glass was not arsenic. It was the residue of a tablet of aspirin. There was arsenic, but it must have been added in a liquid form. Now when I learned that I sent a man to make an intensive search for an empty bottle small enough to go into a man's pocket or a woman's hand-bag. It was a hundred to one chance, but it was in our favour that the Corporation dust carts don't go beyond the railway bridge. The Armours have to dispose of their own rubbish. The gardener burns some of it, and what cannot be burned is buried in a hole at the end of the garden. My man went through all the stuff that has been dumped there lately. He found one of those little oval bottles that hold aspirin or cascara tablets, the fourpenny halfpenny size. It had been washed out but the stopper betrayed the fact that it had held arsenic. Mark Armour bought a bottle of aspirin, that size, at Lukin's, the chemist in Market Square on his way to Brighton, the day before his sister died. He's got that still."

Raynham's cigarette had gone out. He threw it into the fire. "Circumstantial," he said. "It's not positive proof. I suppose your theory is that he took this bottle with him to the doctor's and helped himself to arsenic in the dispensary during the few minutes he was there alone?"

"It's a theory that covers the facts in our possession, Mr. Raynham. As I said before, I'm sorry. I'm not enjoying this case, but I've got to do my duty. I'm sorry for—"

He stopped. Raynham knew he had been going to say "your niece." He was thinking of Lucy too. A murderer. How was she to be spared the shock of knowing that to be a certainty? But was it certain?

"You have not convinced me yet," he said. "Where does Armour keep this bottle of aspirin? When was the house searched?"

"While they were at the funeral, all but the elder brother George and an old woman who lives just over the bridge and is working for them now the maids have left. The bottle was on his dressing-table."

"Then anyone in the house might have walked into his room and taken it. One of the maids, one of his sisters. That's in his favour, Brisling. What about finger-prints?"

"Nothing clear. The label covers most of the glass."

"And on the tumbler found on the bedside table?"

"Oh, they're clear enough. The cook who admittedly brought it up from the pantry where she filled it from a sealed bottle of milk from Henslowe's dairy. There's her finger and thumb. The other prints are those of the dead woman. But there was no need for the murderer to touch the glass."

"True. Have you asked him about it?"

"No. The coroner will at the adjourned inquest. We shall see how he reacts. I need hardly ask you to keep this to yourself, Mr. Raynham."

"I understand. When does the coroner resume his enquiry?"

"The day after to-morrow."

"And will it be concluded?"

"I think so. If there's a verdict against Armour we shall arrest him then and there, naturally."

"And if it's some person or persons unknown?"

Brisling laid down his pen. "It's a fearful responsibility," he said gloomily. "Look here, Mr. Raynham, I can guess how you feel about this. It must be difficult for you to take a dispassionate view—but—honestly—have you any real doubt of this wretched young man's guilt?"

Raynham's reply was emphatic. "I certainly have. His sisters had equally good opportunities to commit the crime—and a motive wasn't lacking in either case, as I daresay you know."

Brisling looked at him. "You don't suggest they were all in it together?"

"No. I think we can rule that out. You'll have to make your choice, Brisling."

The superintendent sighed. "Well, I may give him a bit more rope, though I don't see much chance of any more evidence bearing on the case coming in now. Look here, Mr. Raynham, about—about a certain young girl in whom you are interested, if you take my advice you will get her away now—at once. If she's abroad she'll be well out of the business. If she's here she may be drawn into it. Even if she isn't the strain on her will be great."

"Thank you," said Raynham. "I'll do my best. You're right, of course. I can't tell you how I dread the immediate future for her sake. The trouble is that she's loyal. I'm afraid she may insist on staying."

"How old is she?"

"Eighteen."

"What about parental authority?" enquired the superintendent.

"You mean that I may have to tell my brother-in-law the facts? I can't do that without her leave. She may consent to go to save him pain. He's so perfectly unconscious, and being on the local Bench makes it worse. It would be a fearful shock for him."

"On the other hand if he's left in ignorance, and he is one of the magistrates who commit Armour for trial on the capital charge how is his daughter going to feel about that?"

"Ghastly!" said Raynham. "However you look at it it's bad."

"They'll have to be told, he and the aunt," said Brisling. "Then they can all go abroad for the winter, alleging his or her health as an excuse, and shut up their house or let it. When they come back it'll all be over. Or—in the Colonel's place—I'd sell the house and settle down somewhere else. A clean break."

"If human beings could be moved about like pieces on a board," said Raynham, "wood or ivory—but they're flesh and blood. It won't be so easy. And as to parental authority—have you any children of your own, Superintendent?"

"No."

"I thought not. Well, I'm much obliged to you. I'll do my best. I won't take up any more of your time now."

"That's all right," said Brisling. "I find it helpful talking things over with you, Mr. Raynham. Your experience in the East. Come in again."

CHAPTER XIV
LIFE—AND LUCY

THE PARLOURMAID at Simla smiled a welcome as she stood aside to allow Raynham to pass into the hall.

"We thought you might be coming down for the weekend, sir. Your room's all ready. I'll take your suit-case up. The Colonel and Miss Rivers are both out, but you'll find Miss Lucy in the drawing-room."

That was what Raynham had hoped for. He wanted to have a talk with Lucy before he met her father or her aunt.

The drawing-room at Simla was upstairs and from the window one could look across the narrow strip of common land and the parade to the sea. Lucy had been watching the grey green line of water stealing in over the wet sands almost in silence under a still and leaden sky. She turned with a quick, startled movement that betrayed nervous tension as her uncle entered.

"Oh, Geoffrey! Have you—?"

"Come and sit by the fire, Lucy."

"Have you found out anything?"

He came to the point at once. "I've gone into things a bit. You can't do any good by staying on here, Lucy. I want you to let me take you away to-morrow. I'll fix it with your father."

"You mean without telling him about—about me and Mark?"

"Yes." He paused for a moment. "There is just this. He is on the bench of magistrates here. If Armour is arrested it will probably fall to him to commit him to trial. You are prepared to face that, Lucy?"

She passed the problem of her future relations with her father as irrelevant. "You really think that Mark will be arrested?" her voice shook.

"I'm afraid it will come to that."

"He didn't do it! Surely they'll believe him."

"Lucy," said Raynham earnestly. "If I can help him I will. It won't help him to have you drawn into this. You can't imagine what it would be like. Newspaper men trying to interview you. People staring and pointing you out. Your father—he's an old man—I don't know how he'd stand it."

"But why should I be drawn into it?"

"You might not be, but there's a risk. Superintendent Brisling advises you to go away."

"Superintendent—" She flushed painfully. "Does he—"

"He knows. Don't mind too much. He's quite a good sort."

He saw that that had gone far to break down her resistance.

She shivered. "What do you want me to do then?" she asked faintly.

He touched her hand. "My dear—I suggested India the other day—but I think that is too far. I doubt if your father would consent. An old friend of mine is going to Rome next week. She would be delighted to have you as her companion. You could join her in London to-morrow. You need a few days for passport formalities. Leave it to me."

"They are just coming in," she said hurriedly. "I hear Daddy's voice in the hall. I—I don't want him to be hurt."

There was no time for more. Mary Rivers and the Colonel greeted Raynham cordially. Both were in good spirits. The Colonel had enjoyed a round of golf, and Mary a game of bridge at her club.

"Is your head better, Lucy darling? This child has been suffering from neuralgia, Geoffrey. We've had the doctor for her and he's prescribed a tonic. I hope you take it regularly."

"Yes, Aunt Mary."

"She looks a bit off colour," said Raynham. "I think a thorough change might be a good thing. Why not let her go to Italy with Octavia Allardyce, John? You remember Octavia? She's a widow now. She was telling me the other day she wished she knew a nice girl she could take with her. Florence, Rome, perhaps a peep at Sicily. You'd like that, wouldn't you, Lucy? What about it, John? I mean it."

The maid had brought in tea. Miss Rivers, very upright, was pouring out. "Lucy has never been away from home except to school."

"Well, she's got to begin some time."

The Colonel glanced at his sister doubtfully. "What do you say, Mary?"

Miss Rivers answered emphatically. "Very kind of you to think of it, Geoffrey, but Lucy is too young. I'm sure Mrs. Allardyce wouldn't care to assume such a responsibility. Men don't realise. Lucy is a home bird. You don't want to go, do you, dear?"

"I—not specially, Auntie. Will you have some bread and butter, Geoffrey?"

Raynham took a slice from the proffered plate and bit into it savagely. The Colonel did not disguise his satisfaction.

"That's a good thing. Frankly, I couldn't spare her. The one ewe lamb, eh? But I'll take you abroad myself next summer if you hanker after foreign parts, Lucy. A week at lovely Lucerne, what? And meanwhile persevere with that tonic and take more out-door exercise."

Raynham was silenced. He had been unprepared for such determined opposition. For the moment there was nothing more to be done, especially as Lucy had failed to back him up. He glanced at her reproachfully. She avoided his eye. He was beginning to be irritated by the Colonel's complete unconsciousness of anything amiss. He loved his child. How could he remain so blandly unaware of her unhappiness? And Mary Rivers, too, thinking of nothing but her bridge winnings. How dared she talk about responsibility! He set down his empty cup. "Well, what about a spot of exercise now? Come for a walk along the beach with me, Lucy?"

He had expected a refusal, but she got up at once. "I'd like it."

Five minutes later she joined him in the hall.

"It looks like rain," he warned.

"It doesn't matter. I've nothing on to hurt." She was wearing a coat of rough brown frieze and a red cap drawn over her honey coloured hair. The little face with its pointed chin looked very wan in the failing light of the October afternoon. She did not speak again until they were crossing the common.

"You're not angry with me, Geoffrey?"

"I am, rather. Why didn't you say you were dying to go?"

"I should have been," she said wistfully, "if I'd had the chance a few months ago. Italy! Daddy and Aunt Mary are perfectly happy here, but I think it's deadly dull. I've longed to get away. Italy was one of my dreams. But now I should be thinking about Mark all the time. I don't think I could bear it."

They had reached the parade, deserted at that hour, and were walking towards the last shelter beyond which the asphalt pavement ended and the sand dunes began. Involuntarily she glanced down at the beach. There she had sat with Mark in the sheltering darkness.

"Geoffrey—you haven't seen him, have you?"

He stopped to light a cigarette where the shelter broke the wind. "As a matter of fact, Lucy, I have. He's remarkably good looking, of course. I daresay—" For an instant he hesitated. Should he be brutal? It might be the kindest way in the end. "I daresay a good many women have fallen in love with him."

"He's never cared for anyone before me," she said defensively.

"Perhaps not. On the other hand it's been his business to make himself agreeable to women, even, if they wanted it, to make love to them."

"What do you mean?"

"Has he never told you what his job was? I see he hasn't. He was a professional dancing partner. Last year he was taken to le Touquet and on to the Lido by one of his patronesses. The year before there was someone else. His face was his fortune. My dear, I hate to hurt you, but it's better to know the truth."

They had reached the end of the parade and turned back. The wind had risen and was behind them now, helping them along.

"You haven't hurt me," she said. "I don't care one little bit. He's been miserable always. He had to live somehow. He didn't cheat. He gave them their money's worth. That's all there was to it. I—I don't mind."

After a moment she added in a hard voice, "If you're against him we'd better stop talking about this."

"I'm not, Lucy. I liked what I saw of him. But I have to think of you and your happiness."

"I know. I do appreciate your kindness. I had no one to turn to. I don't want to be taken away, but I do want you to stay and help me. I believe I ought to tell Daddy that Mark and I are engaged. That might be of some use, but it's difficult because—"

"Armour never actually asked you to marry him?"

She admitted that he had not. "He said it was impossible. Of course, I knew he was poor. Oh, I don't know what to do."

"Keep out of it if you can!" said Raynham. "For his sake as much as your own."

"All right," she sighed, "but I won't go away. We must go home now. Daddy won't like it if we're late for dinner."

CHAPTER XV

SUSPENSE

CLAIRE WAS LIGHTING the gas in the hall when Mark came in. "Where on earth have you been all this time?" Her voice was sharp with irritation. "Nannie had to go at three as usual. I don't think I ought to be left alone for hours with those two. I mean—"

"I'm sorry, Claire. I didn't know you'd mind. George is all right, isn't he? I simply couldn't stick it here any longer so I went to the pictures. I hoped the din would stun me and it did pretty well for a bit."

Claire blew out her taper and replaced it in the drawer of the hall stand. "The pictures! Good Heavens! It'll be all over the town. Ten days after Bertha's funeral."

"Does it matter? They can't say anything worse than they're saying already."

"What are they saying?"

He looked at her quickly and looked away again. "We shall be the last to hear, naturally, but it must be pretty bad or dear old Nannie wouldn't be so affectionate."

"I know," said Claire. "She always called us duckie and brought us sweets when she felt there was going to be a row over something we'd done. Come into the draw-ing-room, Mark. I want to talk to you. There's a fire. I've had a fire there every day since—wouldn't Bertha be hor-rified! She always said it was nonsense feeling the cold. If you ran about making yourself useful you wouldn't. I can hear her saying it."

"Don't!" said Mark. "I'm going to put my feet on the fender and she wouldn't have liked that either. We'll never get away from her in this house."

"I wanted to speak to you about that," she said. "I suppose we can sell the place now and divide the money? I want to get right away."

"What about George and Winnie?"

"George would be all right in a doctor's family where they take slight mental cases. He'd be happy anywhere with a paste pot and a constant supply of picture papers. I don't know about Winnie—but I'm not going to spend the rest of my life looking after her, Mark."

"No, of course not."

"We ought to tell the local agents."

"Yes."

"I want to get right away!" she said again feverishly. "It's so awful being shut up here with those two—and the fact that, in a way, I'm fond of them both makes it worse. If I didn't care twopence about Winnie I shouldn't feel so ashamed when she makes an exhibition of herself, poor thing."

"She's not been down to Cardew's again?" Mark said quickly.

"No. But if she'd made up her mind to go I couldn't have stopped her. She was afraid of Bertha, but she doesn't mind me. I've no influence. She's sitting in her bedroom writing poetry."

"I suppose she realises that she'll have to go with us to the inquest to-morrow? Are you ready to say your piece, Claire? We shall all be called this time. It's inevitable."

She shivered. "It's turning colder, I think. It will be just the questions the police have asked already, won't it?"

"I suppose so. But coroners can butt in on their own and go into things that wouldn't be admitted as evidence in a law court. They can be beastly. Well"—he lit a cigarette—"We've got to go through it. I daresay we're all dreading it. I ordered a taxi to fetch us from Thorn's Garage. Nannie'll be here to look after George. It may last all day."

"It's like looking forward to an operation without anaesthetics," she said.

"It is rather," he agreed. "That's why I went to the pictures. There's a French proverb that meets the case. *La journée sera longue, mais elle finira.*"

"Where did you hear that?" she asked curiously.

"I remember seeing it written on the flyleaf of one of mother's books."

"Poor mother!" sighed Claire. "I wonder what became of her. I wonder if she's still living." She looked up at the clock.

"Seven. I must go and make the cocoa. Will you fetch George and see that he washes his hands? He always gets out of it if he can."

Mark threw the end of his cigarette into the fire and stood up. "Another ghastly meal to sit through. Oh, hell! There's a bottle of whisky in the sideboard. I think I shall take it up to my room afterwards and see if I can't get dead drunk."

"Really, Mark?"

"Yes, really."

"I wouldn't if I were you. It won't help you to have a blinding headache to-morrow."

"I suppose you are right."

Claire made the cocoa over the gas ring in the kitchen and carried the jug into the dining-room before she went upstairs to tell Winnie that supper was ready. Her heart sank as she knocked at her half-sister's door. She might find Winnie limp, dishevelled, crying and moaning on her bed. But the voice that bade her come in sounded cheerful.

"Hullo, Claire. Be careful how you step."

Winnie was kneeling on the floor surrounded by paper patterns and fragments of pale blue silk.

"You don't remember this dress? I had it years ago when skirts were long and full. There's heaps of material. I'm cutting a jumper out of it. I had to put the candle on the floor to see." Winnie always did her dressmaking by fits and starts and at the most inconvenient moments, but as her efforts to make new garments out of old ones seemed to make her happy her family were careful not to discourage them. Claire, inwardly hoping that the latest creation would not be finished in time to shock the coroner, said that she liked that shade of blue.

"So do I," said Winnie dreamily. "They say you should match your eyes. Claire, it's all right about Ian Cardew. I thought of it in the night. Of course, I thought, he's Scotch, and Scotchmen are cautious. He's simply waiting until all this has blown over. Then he'll come forward and declare himself. We'll be married quietly. You shall be my bridesmaid. Don't you think I'm right about Ian?"

"I—I expect you are," said Claire. At any rate the illusion would give them a breathing space. "Supper is ready. Winnie—you know the inquest is to-morrow? The papers came this morning. Mark has ordered a taxi to take us."

"Has he?" Winnie was collecting the pins scattered over the carpet. "I'll be down in a minute. Claire, if there's enough stuff do you think a sort of jabot frill would improve this? I do love this blue. It wouldn't suit you. You're too dark. Do you think I need go to this inquest?"

"I'm afraid you'll have to. It's—it's a sort of legal summons," said Claire.

"All right. But it seems so silly."

CHAPTER XVI

SPITE

A BESPECTACLED young woman with a plain, earnest face took Raynham's card and ushered him into her employer's room.

"Mr. Glide is expecting you."

The wizened little man seated at the roll-top desk rose and offered a frail and bony hand. "Sit down, Mr. Raynham. Inspector Collier, of the Criminal Investigation Department at Scotland Yard, rang me up a few minutes ago and told me you would be calling. I should always do my utmost for a friend of his, but I ought to warn you that I don't undertake any and every case."

"Quite. I understand that. I've been doing a bit myself. But my position is rather a difficult one. It's the Dennyford poisoning mystery. I've been staying down there with relatives."

"One moment. I remember something in the papers at the time. A Miss Armour, wasn't it? She died about a fortnight ago? There was an inquest adjourned for further enquiries."

"It's being resumed to-morrow morning."

"Is there a suspect?"

"Yes. Her half-brother. The local superintendent seems convinced of his guilt. I am not."

"What was the poison?"

"Arsenic."

"Is there any evidence of how it was administered?"

"Yes. She was in the habit of drinking a glass of milk either at her bed-time or when she woke up in the night. The doctor who was called in to attend her had his suspicions and took possession of the empty glass. There was a sediment at the bottom which proved to be aspirin, but analysis also revealed traces of arsenic."

"Any finger-prints?"

"Those of the dead woman and those of the cook whose duty it was to take the milk up to her mistress's room every night. No others."

"Well—there'd be no need to handle it." Glide took a lump of grey modelling wax from his desk and fingered it thoughtfully. "That narrows the field of enquiry, doesn't it. Someone who knew her habits and who had access to the house during that evening. It ought not to be too difficult. What does the household consist of?"

"A half-witted brother of the dead woman and a sister who is slightly mad, and a step-brother and sister, the children of a second wife. The first wife died in an asylum."

"What's their social status?"

"Oh, middle class, I suppose. The father was a retired manufacturer from the Midlands. But they weren't visited. There have been several scandals. The second wife was the governess, a French girl, and the old man married her only a few weeks after the death of the first wife. Shock number one. Then after a few years, during which I'm afraid the poor woman was very miserable, she bolted with the French master at a prep. school in the town. Shock number two. Then when Mark, her boy, was about seventeen, and just leaving school, he forged his father's name on a cheque and was turned out of doors. I understand that he joined up when the War started a few weeks later. He wasn't seen again in Dennyford until this summer. Meanwhile the father had died leaving everything to his eldest daughter for her life, the property to be divided equally among the survivors at her decease. While she lived they were absolutely dependent on her."

Glide grunted. "And they all lived together, snapping and snarling, eh? Family life is sacred, I don't think! How many servants living in?"

"The cook and a housemaid."

"Take one from six. It sounds like a simple subtraction sum. Are these people friends of yours, Mr. Raynham?"

"No."

Raynham had known that Lucy's name would have to be brought in sooner or later. He went on with his narrative, touching on her infatuation for the suspected man and describing the steps he had taken up to date. Glide listened attentively, his brown eyes very bright under the overhanging brows, his restless fingers busy with his lump of wax.

"It looks bad for the young man," he said at last. "That business of the empty aspirin bottle found on the rubbish heap supplies just the kind of circumstantial evidence that impresses a jury. I don't say that it's without its effect on me. It certainly sounds as if he were guilty. One feels a lurking sympathy. She was the nagging type of woman that rasps a man's nerves. Probably he didn't realise what a painful and lingering death it would be. Don't misunderstand me. I hold no brief for murderers. If he did it he'll have to swing. I wouldn't lift a finger to save him."

"If it can be proved beyond a doubt Lucy may get over it," said Raynham. "If he's condemned on no more evidence than they've got now she'll go on believing him innocent, and her life will be ruined. She'll devote herself to his memory."

"It would have been better to get her away from the place," said Glide.

"I know. She won't go. It may be misplaced chivalry on her part, but—well, the rats that leave the sinking ship are prudent animals, but one doesn't admire them specially. I've tried to dissuade her, but I think all the more of her for sticking to him."

"What does he say about it?"

"He hasn't written or attempted to see her since the inquest was opened. That looks bad, I suppose."

Glide was silent for a moment. "What do you want me to do?"

"To supplement the police inquiries by private investigation."

"It won't be easy. I shall have no official standing and no help from the family. I can't make bricks without straw. I tell you what I'll do. I'll attend the adjourned inquest to-morrow, and when that is over, if there's still any doubt and I think I can be of any use in solving it I'll carry on."

"Thank you. I'll ask the superintendent to give you a good seat."

"I like the front row of the gallery if there is one. I hope the super isn't an anti-Glide. The police are rather divided in their minds about me. Shall I see you afterwards?"

"Why not come down with me now and meet Brisling? We must keep on the right side of him. The enquiry opens at ten to-morrow."

"Very well." Glide gave some instructions to his secretary. He kept a suit-case ready packed in a cupboard. Within ten minutes they had left his office, and they reached Dennyford about eight o'clock, having had dinner on the train.

They went straight to the police station and found the superintendent still in his room. He received them civilly though without any display of enthusiasm.

"I've heard of you, Mr. Glide. I'm not going to say I approve of what I've heard about your methods. You want to be present at the inquest to-morrow? No difficulty about that. Will you sit with Mr. Raynham?"

"No. Mr. Raynham wants to keep in the background if he can."

"You know the reason, Brisling," said Raynham.

The superintendent stroked his chin. "It's a pity you couldn't induce that young lady to go away for a while. It may turn out very awkward, her father being a magistrate. I don't know that Mr. Glide's intervention is going to be very helpful. Excuse my being quite frank."

Glide's smile was disarming. "I think I can promise not to get in your way."

A tall young policeman opened the door. "Miss Watts, sir. She says she wants to make a statement."

"One moment." Brisling turned to the others. "That's the cook from the White House. A very important witness. I had a notion she might be keeping something back. I can rely on your discretion, gentlemen? Good. Will you sit a little farther back? I want her here where the light falls on her face. All right, Collins. Show her in." Emily Watts was a big-boned, heavily-built woman with a broad, red face and an ill-tempered mouth. She was rather too smartly dressed in a bright blue coat lavishly trimmed with cheap fur, opening over a blue silk frock and ropes of pearls. But her face was not painted, and she looked what she was, a farmer's daughter, unused to the finicking ways of the town bred.

She sat down heavily and went straight to the point.

"I've come to tell you who poisoned Miss Armour."

Brisling drew a writing pad towards him. Neither of the two other men moved.

"You have some fresh information?"

"Well, I've known it all along, but I didn't care to say. But when he—I won't be treated like dirt for anyone. So I came on here and I'll thank you to take it down."

"I'm doing that, Miss Watts, and, as you see, there are two witnesses."

"That's right. Well, then, it was the gardener." Her chair creaked as she leant back in it. Raynham bit his lip. That possibility had occurred to him also. It had probably been contemplated by the superintendent.

Brisling eyed his informant thoughtfully. "Tom Lee? He had the run of the kitchen, I suppose? In and out pumping water and cleaning boots?"

"Yes. He could have slipped into the pantry easily any evening and dropped something into Miss Bertha's glass of milk. It would be standing on the shelf waiting for me to take it up."

"Just so. Did you see him coming from the pantry that evening?"

"No."

"Well, where's your evidence?"

"There was a tin of weed killer down in the potting-shed, wasn't there? And he had a motive for getting rid of Miss Bertha."

"What was that?"

"He was afraid of getting the sack if Miss Bertha found out about his goings on with her sister."

"Which sister?"

"Miss Claire. They used to meet at night in the shrubbery. They were both in it if you ask me, and I'd put them in the dock together. And if I was on the jury they wouldn't have to wait long for my verdict."

The three men watched the angry red face and working mouth gravely. It was clear that Claire Armour would have no mercy shown her in that quarter. The superintendent leaned forward.

"He walked out with you two or three Sundays after he first came to the place, didn't he?"

"How did you know that?"

"It was a guess. Well, you won't be on the jury, Miss Watts. You'll be in the witness-box giving evidence on oath. The truth and nothing but the truth. Have you nothing more definite to tell us? Hearsay and supposition are no use."

"I didn't see either of them putting poison in the milk, if that's what you mean. They weren't such fools as to do it in front of me. I'll be getting on since I'm not wanted. Some folks are born lucky, aren't they! Tom Lee must be one of them. Fancy getting off with a murder under the very noses of the police."

"No one has got off yet, Miss Watts," said Brisling sternly. "I advise you to be careful."

"Me?" Her high colour faded, leaving her a greyish yellow. Glide slipped out of the room and came back with a glass of water. She drank and set the glass down with a hand that shook perceptibly. "You gave me a turn," she said resentfully, "talking to me like that."

"I'm sorry," said Brisling. "Would you like me to ring up a taxi to take you home to your sister's?"

"No. I'm all right now. I can walk."

He went out with her but came back immediately. "Spite, of course," he commented. "There isn't an atom of evidence against those two to put in the balance against the empty aspirin bottle, but she'll drag what she calls the goings on into the light of day. The youngest Miss Armour—you've seen her, Mr. Raynham—she's damned good looking, like her brother, and she's wasted the best years of her life shut up in that house. Poor thing."

He looked at his watch. His visitors took the hint and stood up to go.

CHAPTER XVII
THE MISSING WITNESS

THE PILLORY, thought Mark, with words instead of stones raining down on one's defenceless head. Heavy, sharp-edged words that cut and bruised. Arsenic. Arsenic. A painful death. Yes, very painful. Over two grains. "I mustn't stop my ears. I'd like to hurl that inkstand at the Coroner. Why does he wear that beastly straggling moustache? A moustache like that is an outrage. Oh God! I've got to be careful."

He stood up as his name was called, and walked over to stand by the Coroner's table, facing the jury. He heard excited whispering among the people packed in the narrow space at the back of the court. Someone hissed. The Coroner glanced up quickly.

"Silence!"

The crowd was suddenly quiet. Mark took a dingy black-bound Bible in his slim brown hands.

"I swear before Almighty God—"

"Will you tell us in your own words what happened on the night of the twenty-third? "

"Well, my sister, Bertha, was taken ill, but I didn't know it. My sister Claire woke me between six and seven and told me and I got up then."

"You are a good sleeper?"

"Not particularly, but I happened to have a headache and I had taken a couple of aspirin."

"You keep aspirin by you?"

"Yes, generally, I think."

"You opened a new bottle that night, didn't you?"

"Did I? Very likely. I don't remember."

"Come, your memory can't be as bad as that. You bought a small bottle of aspirin, the four-penny size, at Marshall's in the High Street on the twenty-second."

"I may have done. But what has this to do with my sister's death?"

"I am here to ask questions, Mr. Armour, not to answer them. You had a bottle before that one and finished it. What became of it?"

"I haven't the least idea."

"Is this it?"

"I don't know. It may be. I usually buy that size. What of it?"

"I would advise you not to take that tone with me, Mr. Armour. This bottle was found in the rubbish pit at the bottom of your garden, among the household refuse thrown there during the previous week, on the twenty-sixth of last month. It was subjected to chemical tests and proved to have held liquid arsenic."

Mark's face was white. Beads of sweat stood out on his upper lip. But he answered steadily. "I know nothing about that."

"Did you see your sister before she died?"

"No."

"How was that?"

"She didn't ask for me. I don't think anyone realised that she was dying."

"Were you on good terms with her?"

"Not very."

"How was that?"

"She was rather exacting and inclined to find fault. She often said very bitter things. She flicked one on the raw."

"You were financially dependent on her?"

"I was lately."

"You came in very late that night, after the rest of the household had retired?"

"Yes."

"Where had you been?"

"Oh—just walking about."

Brisling who was standing behind the Coroner's chair, bent over and said something in an undertone. The Coroner nodded.

"Well, I won't press that. What were you about when the cook saw you cross the landing to your own room?"

"I thought I heard somebody moving about below. I went down the backstairs to make sure."

"You were fully dressed?"

"Yes."

"At twenty minutes to three. When did you get in?"

"Oh, before one."

"What were you doing during that hour and a half?"

"I wasn't sleepy. I read a book."

"You could have read in bed?"

"I don't care about doing that with a candle. There's no gas upstairs at White House."

"After the cook saw you you undressed, took a couple of aspirin, and slept so soundly that you did not hear the deceased calling out a few minutes later though the cook heard her from the floor above."

"That is correct."

The Coroner's pen scratched over the paper. For a moment there was no other sound in the crowded court room. To Glide, looking down from his place in the gallery, it seemed that a shadow fell on the witness, the shadow of the gaunt tree whose fruit has accursed.

The Coroner looked up. "That will do for the present, Mr. Armour. I call Emily Watts."

Mark Armour went back to his seat between his two sisters. His self-control had been perfect, but Glide noticed that after a minute he took his handkerchief from his sleeve and wiped his forehead.

Meanwhile the name of Emily Watts had been called three times and had evoked no response. A police sergeant went round to speak to Gladys Pierce who was sitting just behind her former employers. "Where's Miss Watts?"

"How should I know?"

"You were in service together."

"Yes, but we left. I've hardly seen her since."

"All right."

The sergeant went back to Brisling who conferred with the Coroner.

The latter addressed the jury. "The witness may have mistaken the date. We will adjourn for an hour for lunch while she is brought here."

Glide glanced back at the solid mass of humanity wedged between him and the gallery door. Most of his neighbours, he remarked, had come prepared for a long sitting with packets of sandwiches. There was no hope of getting back to his seat again if he left. On the other hand he might be missing a good deal if he remained. He looked down once more into the well of the court. The witnesses had been shepherded into a room on the right. The jury had filed out by another door. Brisling and the sergeant had both vanished. Glide stood up and began the process of pushing past the knees of the other occupants of the front row.

The exit from the gallery was at the back of the building. He saw a parked row of cars, Raynham's the third from the end, and Raynham himself in the driver's seat. Raynham beckoned to him.

"I've offered to go and fetch her. Jump in."

"I thought you were going to keep out of it," said Glide as they turned the corner.

"I know. But if I can be useful to the police they are all the more likely to stretch a point for me. I wonder why she hasn't turned up? She seemed keen enough last night. I don't believe she could have mistaken the date. She knew it was this morning. What are the beds like at the Station Hotel?"

"Lumpy," said Glide briefly. "I wonder if Brisling told off one of his men to follow her home."

"Last night? I shouldn't think so. Good Heavens! You don't suppose—"

"You never know," said Glide. "She talked. Some people might think she talked too much."

They had turned another corner and were on the Marine Parade, a strip of common and the sea on their right, and on their left a long row of stuccoed houses. In July and August there would have been bathing costumes and towels hanging from the balconies, children running up and down the steps, but in November they had a forlorn and deserted aspect.

"Number seven," said Raynham. "She's been staying with a widowed sister who lets lodgings. I tried to interview her the other day but she shut the door in my face. Will you speak to her while I wait in the car?"

Glide went up the steps to the front door, rang the bell and waited. He listened but heard no sound or movement within. He rang again. After an interval the woman next door came up from her basement.

"If it's Mrs. Smith or her sister you're wanting, Mrs. Smith went away on a visit last week and I think her sister must be away too, for the milk's not been taken in this morning and I haven't heard her moving about."

"Thank you," said Glide. "Perhaps I'd better try the back door."

"You get to it by a passage at the end of the terrace."

Glide returned to the car. "Will you come round to the back with me? I don't like this," he added as they entered the narrow passage between brick walls.

The back premises of number seven differed in no respect from those of its neighbours on either side. There was the same clothes line with two or three ragged dusters pegged out on it, the same unkempt patch of grass flanked by a cinder path leading up to the scullery door. The woman in the next house had come out and was watching them over the low party wall.

A sealed bottle of milk was standing on the scullery window sill, and as they approached, a large black cat emerged from the coal shed and came up to them mewing to rub itself against Raynham's legs. Glide peered through the window.

"The gas is still burning in the room beyond." He tried the door and found it on the latch. "We can't stand on ceremony."

He went in and Raynham followed. They passed through the dark little scullery into the kitchen where the gas jet flared blue in the grey light of the November morning. There was a tin of cocoa on the table and two cups, one full and the other half empty and standing in a pool of spilt liquid. A chair had been knocked over. The body of Emily Watts lay between it and the kitchen stove.

"I was afraid of this," said Glide as he stooped over her. "Poor woman. She's gone to her account."

"Dead?" gasped Raynham.

"And cold. There's a public call box at the corner of the terrace. I noticed it as we came along. Will you ring up Brisling? There's no time to lose. I'll wait here."

"Oughtn't we to search the house at once? The murderer may be lurking on the premises," suggested Raynham.

"He isn't. But if you go out the front way you'll dodge the woman next door. We don't want to embark on explanations before the police arrive."

Raynham hurried off. Left to himself the little inquiry agent stood motionless, looking about him with bright dark eyes, noticing the fur trimmed blue coat Miss Watts had worn when she called at the police station thrown carelessly over the end of the sofa with her hat and gloves, the smear of blood on the polished steel of the fender, the thick brown pool of cocoa on the table, the position of the other chair drawn up to the table.

"Yes," he murmured. "That's important—if Brisling doesn't miss it."

Chapter XVIII
DEATH AT NUMBER SEVEN

The youthful reporter for the *Dennyford Gazette* jumped off his bicycle and pushed his way through the little group of errand boys and women with perambulators that had gathered to stare at the policeman standing on the steps of number seven and the two motor cars and three motor bicycles waiting in the road.

"Can I have a word with the superintendent?"

"No. He's busy."

"It's Mrs. Smith, isn't it?"

"No, her sister, Miss Watts."

Light broke on the reporter. "Gosh! The witness who didn't turn up before lunch! Is that why the inquest has been adjourned again? What's happened to her?"

"Look here," said the constable, "I'm not supposed to talk, and, anyway, I don't know any more than you. I'm here to keep people from pushing in."

"Right." The reporter had seen the woman next door looking through the drawing-room curtains. He knew her slightly, for some friends of his had stayed in her rooms last August. He betook himself to number six.

Meanwhile Raynham and Glide, obeying a thinly-veiled injunction to get out of Brisling's way, had left the gloomy basement kitchen with its silent occupant to the police, and established themselves in the sitting-room on the first-floor. Glide had lit the fire and they sat over it, Raynham smoking cigarettes, the little inquiry agent fingering his lump of modelling wax. At intervals Raynham looked at his watch. He wanted to get back to Lucy, but he must see the superintendent first.

There was coming and going all the afternoon, heavy steps on the stairs, voices, opening and shutting of doors. The police surgeon arrived in a hurry and left again. Someone brought a large camera.

"We set the machine going," thought Raynham, "now it's at work. The wheels turning. All to prove—what?"

Brisling came in to them at last, closing the door after him with the air of a man who did not intend what he was about to say to be overheard.

"You've got a fire? Good. It's deadly cold in that kitchen."

He drew up a chair and sat down heavily. He looked tired and worried. "You two were with me last night and heard her. She left us to go to her death. I blame myself.

The inquest on Miss Armour is adjourned. The luncheon interval wasn't over when you rang me up, fortunately. Doctor Payne was very decent about it. Some Coroners would have been nasty. I've sent a couple of my men in a car to fetch Lee here. Would you like to hear what he has to say for himself?"

"We should," said Raynham. "By Jove! It almost looks as if she was right and it was weed killer after all, doesn't it?"

"I don't know what to think!" confessed the superintendent. "We've got to account for the aspirin bottle."

"Yes," said Glide placidly. "Awkward when you've completed the picture to find some pieces over." It was the first time he had spoken since Brisling had joined them, and something in his tone made them both look at him. He smiled deprecatingly. "Sorry if I'm being tiresome. You haven't moved the cups, I hope, Superintendent?"

"Nothing has been moved," said Brisling rather gruffly.

"Good. It's rather important. I daresay you noticed—"

There was a knock at the door. Brisling raised his voice.

"Is that Collins? Bring your man in here." Raynham moved his chair round so that his back was to the light. He did not think that Lee was likely to identify him with the shabby stranger who had lodged two nights with Mrs. Trant, but he wanted to run no risks.

Lee came forward with unconcealed reluctance and stood before them.

Brisling cleared his throat. "I've sent for you," he began, "because I think you may be able to help me. Miss Watts was formerly your fellow servant. You met her in the town last night, didn't you?"

"I—yes."

"You quarrelled."

"No. It was just outside Plummer's, the tobacconist's. I'd come in to buy a packet of fags just before the shops closed."

"Just so. You were seen talking together by several people."

"I daresay."

"You came here later in the evening."

"No."

"You haven't warned him," said Glide.

"Didn't I? I meant to. You needn't answer any question I ask, Lee. Any statement you make must be voluntary. That's the law."

Glide suppressed a smile. It was so evident that Brisling would have liked to add, "and a damn silly law, too!"

Brisling resumed. "Well—you parted from her outside Plummer's. When would that be?"

"The shop was just closing. A few minutes after seven."

"What did you do then?"

"I rode my bike back to Mrs. Trant's where I lodge."

"A mile out of the town and just this side of the railway bridge. You didn't go out again?"

"I went along to the White House to make up the furnace, like I do every night."

"Can you bring any witnesses to corroborate you?"

"What do you mean?"

"Would Mrs. Trant be able to say she saw you come in and go out again?"

"No."

"How's that?"

"She'd gone out to the pictures. She generally goes once a week."

"And you didn't see Emily Watts again after you left her outside Plummer's?"

"No."

There was a pause. Lee looked from one to the other. He moistened his lips. "What's it all about?"

"Emily Watts is dead."

"Emily? You don't think—"

"Here"—Glide intervened—"it's a shock, isn't it. Have a gasper. The superintendent won't mind. Try one of mine."

He threw Lee his case. The young man caught it mechanically but only to hand it back. "Thank you, sir, but I'd rather not. I'm all right, though it was a bit of a knock out. May I go?"

Brisling nodded. "Yes. But mind your step, Lee." He caught Glide's eye. "Wait in the passage. I'll see you again later."

When the young gardener had gone out of the room he turned to the little man angrily. "Why did you butt in? I can't have that."

"I know. I'm sorry. I yielded to temptation. I wanted to make sure."

"Sure of what?"

"Why, those cups on the kitchen table. The full one wasn't quite full. I fancy the visitor had taken a sip or two. The handle was on the left. Which way would it be if you were drinking?"

Brisling whistled. "I get you!"

"Lee caught my case with his left hand."

"So he did! Well, I'm bothered! They're right about you, Mr. Glide. I don't mind admitting that I might have missed that. Not in the long run, of course, but I hadn't tumbled to it then. I've had a lot to think of. One more scandal! The family's used to them, that's one thing. It lets your young man out, Mr. Raynham. And yet—I don't know." He rubbed his chin uneasily.

Raynham stood up. It was growing late and he wanted to get back to his brother-in-law's house.

"Shall you detain Lee?"

"Yes. I think I shall be justified in doing that. I shan't charge him to-night. He'll be held pending investigations."

"It wasn't murder, you know," said Glide. "Accidental. I'm not sure that he even touched her. She jumped up, caught her foot in the rug. There's a hole in it, and I nearly tripped up myself. In falling she hit her head against the edge of the fender. That accounts for the blood, but it wouldn't have killed her if her heart had been all right. You saw how it was with her last night. You nearly did for her yourself, Superintendent. Her lips turned blue then."

"Agreed," said Brisling, "but why didn't the young fool admit it? Why did he lie in wait for a woman he had no use for and follow her home and accept her invitation to come in and have a cup of cocoa—by gum! That's an idea! That cocoa! We'd better have it analysed! I mustn't waste any more time talking. Come round to the station later on if you like, Mr. Raynham. Good afternoon."

"He does get them!" said Glide with a chuckle as he and Raynham walked down the road in the gathering dusk. A streak of primrose light on the western horizon was all that was left of the day.

"Get what?"

"Ideas."

"You think Lee was trying to prevent the woman from blurting out all she knew about his—his affair with Claire Armour?"

Glide seemed to hesitate. "That's the obvious expla-nation. It fits the facts in our possession—but there may be others. The younger Miss Armour is a very beautiful woman. He was sitting on the bench behind her with the housemaid. I saw him watching her. He's in love with her right enough. No getting over that."

They parted at the gate of Simla. Glide was returning to the Station Hotel. "There's a lot of talk in the bars of these places. I may pick up something useful," he said. They had arranged to go round to the police station together about nine o'clock.

Raynham found Colonel Rivers and his sister and Lucy having tea in the drawing-room. The firelight flickered over the parchment-coloured walls with their framed wa-tercolours and Indian embroideries, and was reflected in the well-rubbed silver of the Georgian tea service. There was a scent of violets. Raynham sank into a low cushioned chair and took the cup Miss Rivers offered him gratefully. The atmosphere of warmth and well-being was soothing. Raynham thought that for a little while at least he might forget the body of Emily Watts lying like a badly stuffed doll on the worn linoleum of the kitchen at number seven, and all the problems that she might have helped to solve if she had lived a little longer. As he took a buttered scone from the dish Lucy brought to him he realised that he had had no lunch. He looked up and met her eyes, hoping that she would understand that his smile was meant to reas-sure. How ill the child looked! Prettier than ever, but as frail as a wind flower.

She had been waiting all day. It would be cruel to pro-long her agony of suspense. His first remark was meant for her though it was addressed ostensibly to her father.

"I attended the second hearing of the inquest on Miss Armour, John."

"You did? I wondered where you'd got to, didn't I, Mary? I didn't know you had such morbid tastes. You'd much better have come for a round with me, though it was too misty this afternoon to see the ball. We had a game of bridge instead at the club house. What was the verdict?"

"The inquest was adjourned."

"What, again? Dear me! Is that Brisling? He was round here the other day trying to get me to sign a warrant. I told him to go elsewhere. I don't want to be mixed up in the business. I didn't know you were interested, Geoffrey, but I suppose it's more or less in your line."

"Rather less than more," said Raynham, "but I am following this up." He paused a moment. "There was an unexpected development."

"Really?" It was Mary who spoke. "Would anything be unexpected in that quarter? It really is a terrible family, Geoffrey. They're simply awful. Those that aren't mad are bad, and that's all about it. Can't we find a pleasanter subject of conversation?"

"May I have a second cup of tea?" He shot a warning look at Lucy, who had seemed about to speak, and helped himself to another scone.

"One of the maids who was to have given evidence failed to turn up. Both the maids left after Miss Armour's funeral. I understand that they gave out that they were afraid to remain. This one was staying with a widowed sister who lets lodgings on the Marine Parade. She's been alone there for the sister is away on a visit to friends. Her name was called and as there was no reply she was sent for in the luncheon interval. She was found lying dead in the kitchen."

"Good gracious!" said Miss Rivers.

The Colonel, who had taken up *The Times*, laid it down again. "Dead! You don't mean—"

"Well, there'll have to be an inquiry."

"Was her evidence likely to be important?"

"It might have been."

The Colonel got up and stood on the hearthrug with his back to the fire in the attitude dear to the head of a household about to lay down the law.

"There you are! These chaps are all alike. Can't let well alone. You remember that fellow with a rather similar name—Armstrong. Successful in getting rid of his poor wife, but must needs try it on again, and so fitted the rope round his own neck. If young Armour has been fool enough to tamper with a witness and it can be proved no power on earth will save him."

"They are detaining the gardener, though they aren't charging him," said Raynham.

"The gardener? Rubbish! What's the gardener to do with it!" Miss Rivers cried out. "Lucy! darling!"

Lucy made no answer. She slid sideways from her chair and lay, a little pitiful huddled heap, at her father's feet.

The Colonel was too startled to move. It was Raynham who stooped over her. "Poor child. She is not well."

He picked her up and carried her to her room.

CHAPTER XIX

THE SECRET OF CLAIRE

TO THE TWO MEN coming from the raw cold of the night the Superintendent's room seemed warm to the point of fugginess and almost too brightly lit. Brisling received them with more graciousness than he had shown when they had parted. He had been tired then and exasperated. Since then there had been no opportunity for rest, but he had had a hurried meal and had, to use his own phrase, "cleaned up some of the mess."

"We've got Lee here in the cells and have sent a message to his landlady that she needn't expect him home to-night. I've verified one point. She was at the pictures with her friend last night. The box-office girl saw them go in and the commissionaire noticed them leaving after the show hurrying to catch the last bus. So Lee may have been home as he says—or he may not. And there's the cocoa. I shall know about that before long. I can't keep the fellow indefinitely without charging him—what is it now, Collins?"

The young constable edged his way a little farther into the room. His round boyish face betrayed his consciousness that these were stirring times.

"It's Miss Armour, sir. She says she must see you."

"Good Lord! Which one?"

"The dark one."

"Show her in."

Brisling switched off the unshaded electric bulb that hung from the ceiling and turned on the reading lamp on his desk, tilting the shade so that the light fell on the one unoccupied chair. "Does it remind you of last night, gen-tlemen? My God! That woman's dead."

The three men stood as Claire Armour entered. The superintendent indicated the chair. "Won't you sit down, Miss Armour? Did you wish to see me alone? These are friends of mine. You can rely on their discretion. They are interested indirectly in the mystery of your sister's death."

"I see. It doesn't matter. They can stay if they want to. I've come to ask if it's true that you've arrested Lee?"

"He is detained on suspicion of having had some hand in the death of Emily Watts."

She closed her eyes for a moment as if the light was too much for her. Raynham noticed the length of the thick black lashes and the lovely curves of the long white throat as she lifted her chin, and, pulling off her black beret, shook back her hair. She and her brother had the same heart-searching physical beauty. A dangerous attribute, he thought, with a sigh, and a dangerous age. She wasn't a girl, of course. Past thirty, and bitterly aware of the waste of her youth.

The great dark eyes were open now and fixed on Brisling's attentive face. "He may refuse to speak. It is better you should know the truth. He's my lover. I'm not ashamed of it. We're going to be married as soon as all this is over and we can get away from here." The three men regarded her in silence. They were embarrassed as the average Englishman is apt to be by the revelation of passion. Raynham thought wistfully. "It must be wonder-ful to be loved like that, and by such a woman!" It was an experience that had not come to him. Love, more than once, but never beyond measure.

Brisling spoke at last. "Thank you, Miss Armour. I realise that it hasn't been easy for you to bring yourself to come here and—and speak out. May I ask how you heard of this fresh development?"

"You mean about Emily? Nannie—Mrs. Trant heard, and she came up to the house and told me. She's very upset, of course. Tom lodges with her and she's very fond of him."

Brisling picked up a paper-weight on his desk absently and put it down again. "Does your brother know about you and Lee?"

"No. Not yet."

"You haven't told him, but he might have found out something?"

"I don't think so. I loathe concealment, but we simply had to be careful during my sister's lifetime—and since she died there's been such a lot of worry that I haven't felt equal to facing any fuss."

"You think your brother would make a fuss?"

"No. But Winnie might." A little colour crept into the pale cheeks as she added in a lower key "She's—difficult."

Brisling leaned forward. "Forgive me, Miss Armour. Please don't think I mean to be offensive—but you said just now that you weren't ashamed of your—your relations with Lee. I know that during your elder sister's life you were financially dependent on her. Am I to conclude that you didn't care for Lee sufficiently to marry him and try to make ends meet on his wages?"

"If he'd been sure of getting a job," she said, "but Bertha wouldn't have given him a character. We might have taken the risk. We were thinking of it—but I was afraid of dragging him down. Will you let him go now?"

He looked at her, amazed by her simplicity. Was it possible that she did not realise how damning these admissions were?

"Let him go," he repeated as if considering the matter. "On what grounds?"

She twisted her hands together. "Oh dear, haven't I made it clear? He isn't interested in Emily. He wouldn't think of going to supper or whatever it was, with her."

"That's right, Miss Armour, as far as it goes. He wasn't interested, but she was. When he first came to the White House she annexed him for herself. He went out with her two or three Sundays not very willingly, I fancy. And then—well, she lost him. She was jealous of you, Miss Armour, and she meant to vent her spite this morning at the inquest. She met him yesterday and tried to bargain with him. Failing in that she came here. She was here at this hour last night, sitting in that chair you're in now. She went back to her sister's house. She prepared cocoa for herself and a visitor. She was—attacked—"

Claire cried out. "No, no! That's impossible. Not Tom—"

"Well, if it is impossible he'll be all right," said Brisling. "I'd go home now if I were you, Miss Armour. It's getting late. How did you come?"

"I walked."

The superintendent turned to Raynham. "Would you drive her back?"

"Of course."

Claire's lips were quivering. "You're going to keep him here?"

"For to-night. Don't you worry about that. We won't hurt him. If he's innocent, Miss Armour, his innocence will be proved."

She stood up, pulling on her beret carelessly. They were all three struck by her complete lack of self-consciousness. It had evidently never occurred to her to wonder what impression she was making on them. Her thoughts were all for Lee.

"Can I see him?"

"Better not," said the superintendent. "Thank you for coming," he added and bit his lip, recalling that he had used the same phrase to the other woman. "Good night, Miss Armour."

Raynham, returning within ten minutes, found the superintendent walking restlessly about the room and Glide sitting quietly in his dark corner. Brisling turned to him.

"Well?"

"I took her as far as her gate. She hardly said thank you. She's completely wrapped up in that fellow."

"Another spicy tit-bit for the Dennyford gossips," said Brisling. "How did she strike you? Unusual, eh?"

"Very," said Raynham. "It comes partly from being brought up outside the social pale, I suppose. There's something fine about her, apart from her sheer physical splendour. My God! Fancy keeping a young woman like that cooped up in a Victorian household, unmated. Like feeding a tigress on rice pudding and stewed prunes."

Brisling looked at him. "You think she killed her sister?"

"I didn't say that. I think not. I hope not." Brisling rang his bell. "Has Lee had his supper, Collins?"

"Yes, sir. Bread and cheese and a glass of beer."

"Bring him in here."

The young gardener looked pale and tired. Brisling told him to sit down.

"You've had time to consider your position, Lee. I've a notion that the death of Emily Watts was more or less accidental, and, if I'm right you haven't much to fear. We know her heart was diseased. She had a sort of seizure in this very room last night. We know what you quarrelled about. She'd put her interpretation—the worst—on your relations with Miss Claire Armour."

He half rose from his seat. "It's a pack of lies—" he began.

Brisling stopped him. "That will do," he said sternly. "You can't keep that up. Miss Armour's been here. She's only just left. And she told us everything."

Glide, fingering his modelling wax, nodded approvingly, unnoticed in the shadows. Brisling was playing his fish very cleverly.

Lee was plainly taken aback. "Did she?" he stammered. "Why? What for?"

"She was afraid you might decline to speak—as you have done—with some notion of sparing her—and she realised that attempts to bamboozle the police do more harm than good. The truth can't harm you if you're innocent, Lee."

The young man pushed his hair back from his forehead with a gesture that betrayed fatigue. "I'm all muddled," he murmured. "I'm not much of a hand at talking anyway. Did she—did she say I was to tell you?"

"She was certain that you had nothing to hide. But you needn't speak," Brisling warned him, "there's no compulsion."

"May I smoke?" Brisling nodded, and Lee fumbled in his pockets and produced a packet of cigarettes. They watched him light one. All his movements were curiously gentle and deliberate. That was one of the marks of his calling. He was used to handling young and tender seedlings without bruising them. It did not prove, Raynham reminded himself, that he was incapable of brutality. His sunburnt face was a mask.

"I met Emily last night outside the tobacconist's. She wanted me to take up with her. She always had but I wouldn't. I didn't care about her. She got angry and started threatening what she'd tell the Coroner when he called her to give evidence. I said she could go to hell and I left her. But after a bit, as I was cycling home, I got worried about what she might say. We—we'd been careful, but I suppose she'd been spying and found out things. I thought I might smooth her down a bit and persuade her to hold her tongue, so after I'd had my supper I went to the house where I knew she was staying on the Marine Parade. I went to the back door. She'd only just got in.

"She seemed pleased to see me and she asked me into the kitchen. I said 'Look here, Emily, I'm sorry I was rude to you. I lost my temper.' We got talking in a friendly way and she started to make cocoa on the gas stove. I didn't want any but I didn't like to say no. I didn't want to upset her again. I kept thinking of Claire and what I ought to do. I wanted to get away. I asked her straight out if she'd keep her mouth shut. She said she would on one condition—that I'd give up Claire and marry her. I laughed. I couldn't help it. She said something then. I won't repeat it. I knew if I stayed after that I couldn't keep my hands off her. So I just got up and walked out of the kitchen and came straight home."

"That isn't all, Lee. She caught her foot and fell, didn't she, striking her head against the fender?"

"She was sitting by the table when I went out. I'd just taken one sip of the cocoa. She shouted something after me. A bad word."

"Think again, Lee."

"What's the good of thinking? That's the truth."

"Very well." Brisling rang his bell. "Take him back to his cell, Collins."

CHAPTER XX
A FRESH CLUE

WHEN RAYNHAM CALLED at the station the following morning he was shown directly into the superintendent's office. Brisling waved him to a chair.

"I've just got through some of my routine work. That little sleuth of yours was early on the scent," he remarked.

"Glide?" said Raynham. "I haven't seen him to-day. "

"He was round here before eight to ask if he might have another look round number seven. I let him. He won't find anything. We went through the place with a fine tooth comb yesterday. And anyway I've come to the conclusion that we've got to the bottom of that business. I've had our surgeon's report. Her heart was in a bad state. She's been attending her panel doctor and he says the same. She died a natural death and he's prepared to sign the certificate and avoid another inquest."

"You think Claire Armour and Lee were telling the truth?" said Raynham.

"I do. It all hangs together. Nothing really improbable. I'll admit that at first I thought the murderer of Bertha Armour had struck again. The cook's evidence was an important part of the case I was building up, but I dare say we shall be able to fit a noose round somebody's neck without her help. You can take it from me, Mr. Raynham, that we should make a mistake if we attached too much importance to this second death. It just happened and doesn't affect the main issue. I'm going along to the White House presently with a warrant. There's been enough shilly shally."

"I'm sorry for that," said Raynham.

"You are thinking of your niece," said Brisling bluntly. "Get her away from here before it's too late. Can't you make her see that she'll do him more harm than good if she does get drawn into the case?"

Raynham shook his head. "She feels that to leave would be to desert him. It's not as if she believed him guilty, Superintendent. Can't you wait a little longer? Is your case really strong enough to convince a jury?"

Brisling filled his pipe from a tin on the mantelpiece and lit it before he answered. "The evidence is circumstantial, but it's damning. Listen—"

"I'm listening."

"We can call Gladys Pierce, the housemaid, to prove that Mark Armour habitually kept a bottle of aspirin, the fourpenny size, on his dressing-table. Two days before the murder it was nearly empty. She did not throw it away as there were two or three tablets left. She didn't see that bottle again. There was a new one, nearly full, in its place on the morning after the murder. Gladys is a sharp-eyed, observant young woman, and she is prepared to swear to this. While the family were at the funeral one of my men, carrying out my instructions, searched the rubbish heap at the bottom of the garden and found an empty aspirin bottle, fourpenny size. A subsequent analysis revealed minute but unmistakable traces of arsenic. The bottle had been rinsed in water, but not the stopper. Add to that that Mark Armour was alone in Doctor Cardew's surgery, which adjoins the room where he does his dispensing, a few hours before the crime was committed, and that he was on bad terms with his sister, and dependent on her for everything, and that he benefits from her death."

Raynham sighed. "It sounds bad. And yet— I can't help liking the little I've seen of him. He's not the poisoning type."

"What is the poisoning type?" enquired Brisling cynically.

"Well, whatever else he is, he's the supreme egotist, but what the psycho-analyst said isn't evidence, eh? Here is Glide. I saw him pass the window. He hasn't done much so far," said Raynham. "But one mustn't expect miracles."

"Poor little chap," said the big superintendent good-humouredly, "he's done his level best, I think. We'll have him in."

Glide greeted them cheerfully. He was carrying a small despatch case. He set it down and stooped to the fire, rubbing his bony hands together.

"There's a nip in the air this morning. Well, gentlemen, anything fresh?"

"I was just going to ask you—" began Brisling.

He broke off as the telephone on his desk rang sharply. He took up the receiver. "Hallo! Yes, this is Dennyford police station. Yes, Superintendent Brisling speaking. Oh, thank you very much. I was in a hurry. Yes—"

They saw his face change as he listened. "One moment. I didn't catch—Good Lord! You are sure? Oh, of course. Thank you."

He hung up the receiver.

"Well, I'm damned!" His air of self-confidence had vanished and had given place to bewilderment. "It's the most extraordinary—and sinister—it just shows one can't judge by appearances—"

"For heaven's sake, Brisling, don't keep us in suspense!" cried Raynham. "If it's anything to do with the Armour case—"

"It has. You know those two cups of cocoa we found on the kitchen table at number seven. Lee told us he saw Emily make it and that he had one sup from his cup and that she hadn't begun to drink hers when he left her?"

"Yes."

"I had the contents of Lee's cup transferred to a jar marked number one, and the liquid in her cup and what had been spilled into the saucer was poured into another jar marked two, and sent them off at once by car to the county analyst. Just a matter of form, you know. In fact," he added in a burst of candour, "I might not have done it at all if it hadn't been for a word you let drop, Glide. Because, after all, it was obvious that poison was not the cause of death. But now I hear—he rang me up from his laboratory—there's arsenic enough in number two jar to kill an ox. None in the other." There was a silence in the room as the three men pondered the tremendous significance of these two facts. Brisling produced a handkerchief and mopped his face. "Just in time to save me from dropping a large size brick. This lets out Armour. Lee's our man. He was afraid of getting the sack if Miss Armour found out what was going on. With her death he stood to win a wife and a fourth share of the Armour estate. The motive's all right. But he seemed a simple sort of young fellow to me. I mean, not a bad sort. He must be simple or he wouldn't hope to get away with a second dose of his damned weed killer. There was a tin in the potting shed, you know, but it looked as if it hadn't been opened for months. Well, we've got him. That's one comfort," he sighed.

Glide cleared his throat. "I wonder," he said mildly. "Before you go any farther I'd like to show you something."

He opened his despatch case and produced a quarto sheet of semi-transparent paper on which the outline of a foot was partially traced with indelible blue pencil. He laid it on the desk in front of Brisling.

"This is the outline of the muddy print of a woman's shoe on the flag stone outside the scullery window at number seven. Notice the pointed toe and the shape of the heel. There are other prints between the kitchen door and the coal shed but they are all much larger." He took a brown strap shoe, a good deal trodden over, and a black kid slipper from his case. "The brown shoe belonged to Emily Watts. I found it in her room. The black slipper is her sister's. They both wore sevens. The footprint outside the window was made by a woman wearing a shoe two or three sizes smaller than theirs."

Raynham was silent. He stood looking down at the sheet of paper and the two worn shoes with a sick distaste. The panting quarry, the hounds in full cry. It seemed to him, not for the first time, that the pleasures of the chase were overrated.

The superintendent was less squeamish. He slapped his knee. "Claire Armour! They worked it together! She'd be the moving spirit! She went with him and waited outside.' But we mustn't jump to conclusions. I'll send somebody to photograph that print and take the proper measurements, and have a look at it myself before I go on to the White House."

"What about these shoes?" asked Glide.

"I'll take charge of them and of the drawing." Brisling tried hard to be fair. "I'm obliged to you," he mumbled, "though I should have gone into this matter in any case more thoroughly after getting the analyst's report."

"Isn't it possible," said Raynham, "that there may be some other explanation of this footprint? For instance, the woman next door may have got over the wall and peered into the kitchen either before or after our arrival. She was evidently curious."

"I'll test that," said Brisling. "I'm sorry I can't give you any more of my time just now. I'm going to be busy."

His visitors took the hint.

"I can't help wishing you hadn't found that," said Raynham to Glide when they were outside.

"I thought you wanted the truth."

Raynham groaned. "All right. Carry on. You think those two committed the first murder and attempted the second?"

Glide's wizened little face was very grave. "She's a beautiful woman and what the French call *une grande amoureuse*. It's a pity if it's true, but I'm not sure yet. I haven't begun to think. I'm still collecting facts. The footprint is interesting but perhaps it isn't so conclusive as our friend the superintendent seems to imagine."

"He seems quite sure. I'm afraid he's going to—"

"He's like a bull," said Glide contemptuously. "A clue's a red rag to him. He rushes at it bellowing."

Chapter XXI

ONE IS TAKEN

George had called Claire into the study to show her the last pictures he had pasted into his album. He said nothing, but he pointed out those he considered the prettiest with a stubby forefinger and glanced anxiously at her face to see if she agreed.

"Yes, George, very nice. I like that one. The coloured ones are lovely. And you've put them in straight."

He beamed at her praise. "I'm going on now."

She left him snipping away at the back page of the *Daily Mail*.

As she reached the door he called her back. "Claire!"

"Yes, George!"

Silently, with that pointing finger, he drew her attention to the picture of a stout young woman in a fur- trimmed coat. She read what was printed underneath.

> Emily Watts, an important witness in the White House Poisoning Case, died suddenly yesterday. Below is the house in which her body was found.

"That's right."

"Our Cookie," said George.

"Yes, dear. But I wouldn't put her in your scrap book if I were you. She—she isn't very pretty, is she."

"No," said George indifferently. Emily had never been a favourite of his. He crumpled the sheet and dropped it in his waste paper basket.

Claire was crossing the hall when the door bell rang. She knew Mrs. Trant was busy in the kitchen so she went herself to answer it. Superintendent Brisling was on the step with two large men whom she divined to be policemen in plain clothes.

"I'd be glad of a word with you, Miss. May we come in?"

Claire led the way into the dining-room. "Won't you sit down, please?" she said. She was glad to sit herself, for her knees were trembling and she felt rather sick.

"We'd be glad to know, Miss, what you were doing the night before last. There's no need for you to answer if you'd rather not. It's my duty to warn you that anything you say now might be used against you as evidence."

"Against me? I haven't done anything."

"Then you'll do your best to help us, no doubt," said the superintendent, heavily genial. "Will you tell us what you did the night before last?"

She tried to think. "Nothing particular. We had supper at seven and I cleared it away and laid the breakfast. I went to bed early. I didn't go to sleep. I read a novel. I often do that."

"You did not go out again?"

"No. It was a dark night and raining."

"You didn't—excuse me, Miss, no offence meant— you didn't slip out to meet Lee."

Her pale face flushed but she answered steadily. "No."

"I wonder if you'd mind letting me have one of your shoes just for a minute?"

"One of my shoes? Oh, if you like—"

She stooped to pull one off. It was taken from her by one of the plain clothes men who passed it to his superior officer. Brisling whipped out a little pocket foot-rule and took some measurements of the sole. "Just so," he said. "Well, I'm afraid I've got to ask you to come along with me, Miss Armour. You can pack a suit-case with whatever you may need for a few days. One of my men will go up with you and wait in the passage, and I'll ask you to leave your door open."

"Does that mean that I'm being arrested? What for?"

"For being concerned in an attempt to murder Emily Watts—"

"An attempt!" She stared at him. "Isn't she dead?"

"She's dead enough," said Brisling grimly. "The less you say now the better, Miss. I don't want to take an unfair advantage of you. Where's your brother, Mr. Mark Armour?"

"He's out."

"Go upstairs with her, Evans."

"But I can't leave the house like this. There's Winnie and George—"

"I can't help that, Miss. I'm sorry. I've got to do my duty."

"You're completely mistaken," she said. "I haven't seen Emily since she brought in the breakfast the morning of my sister's funeral. She was a horrible woman, prying and malicious."

"I wouldn't talk now, Miss Armour."

"Oh, all right."

She left the room, Evans following. Five minutes later she came down again in her outdoor things, with Evans carrying a brown paper parcel.

"I'm ready," she said. "I haven't got a suit-case. I've never been away before. May I speak to Mrs. Trant?"

"Yes, Miss."

The three men waited for her in the hall.

"You heard that?" muttered Brisling. "Never been away before. Tied here all her life like a dog to its kennel."

"Couldn't she have run off and earned her living?" argued Evans.

"She wasn't brought up to it."

In the kitchen Mrs. Trant looked up from her egg beating.

"You aren't going out now, Miss Claire? I'm only waiting for Master Mark to come in to make the omelette. Keep an omelette hanging about and you might as well chew the sole of my boot. Is there anything the matter, dearie? Who's that out in the hall? I must be getting deaf. I never heard anyone come in."

Claire went close to the old woman. "Hush! it's the police. They've come to take me away. You'll have to tell Mark, Nannie. Winnie's in her room, but I hadn't the courage to explain to her. You never know how she'll take things, and I couldn't have borne a scene."

"Take you away? You! They've all gone mad, I think. Don't you go, Miss Claire. There's no need."

"I must, Nannie. They—they think I had something to do with the death of Emily. Don't worry about me. They're not unkind."

She went quickly back into the hall, leaving the old woman muttering to herself.

"Whatever next! Whatever next!"

She heard the hall door closed. It was true then. They had taken one of her two away. She was alone in the house with George, who didn't count, and that Winnie, who was about as much use as a wet dish cloth. It was one o'clock, but Mark often came in late for meals. He took long, solitary walks across the muddy fields, avoiding the more frequented footpaths, and coming home limping badly and white with fatigue.

"I used to fancy it might be better with Miss Bertha gone and nobody to nag them, but it don't seem to be," reflected Mrs. Trant. She shook her head dolorously as she thought of Claire. Was it true about her young lady and Lee, she wondered. She was old-fashioned in her ideas. Gentry were gentry, even when they were queer like the Armours, and servants were servants, and both should keep their places. "And if I'd dreamed young Tom would presume I'd have given him what for," she told herself as she strained off the potatoes, spilling half the water on the floor in her agitation.

Winnie Armour put her head round the kitchen door, and, seeing that Mrs. Trant was alone, came into the kitchen.

"Fancy the police coming again!" she said. "I thought I'd keep out of the way until they were gone. It really is too silly. Such a fuss. I suppose it makes them feel important. Where's Claire?"

Mrs. Trant's lips tightened. She had no patience with Miss Winnie and her flighty ways. Strings of beads and a blue scarf tied round her head when she ought to be wearing black for her sister. It wasn't decent.

"They took Miss Claire away with them."

Winnie's round, pale blue eyes grew rounder still. "Took her away? What for?"

"There's Master Mark just come in. I've got to tell him."
Mrs. Trant went into the hall.

"The police came just now and made Miss Claire go
with them," she announced.

"Claire? The damned fools!" he said violently. "What
on earth—did they give any reason?"

"It had something to do with the death of Emily."

"Emily?" His voice betrayed relief. "Her death was natural. Heart failure. Wasn't it? You hear more of what is
being said than we do shut up here."

Mrs. Trant looked at him. "They've got Tom Lee," she
said.

"Our Lee? The gardener? I was wondering why he
hadn't turned up. How does he come into it?"

Winnie began to laugh. "Didn't you know, Mark? How
funny. You and Claire are such pals. I thought you told one
another everything. I thought I was the only one who got
left out of the secrets."

He turned on her so fiercely that she shrank back
against the wall. "What are you cackling about? This is serious. We're all in danger. You can't help it, I suppose. But
you're not a fool, Nannie. If you know anything about Lee
that I don't for God's sake let me hear it before it's too late."

The old woman was trembling. "Oh, my dearie, don't
get so excited. There's no call to upset yourself. Lee went
to see Emily the night she died, and maybe they quarrelled
and that's what brought on the fit or whatever it was."

"But why should Claire be involved?"

Winnie had recovered herself. "They quarrelled about
her, of course. Emily was jealous. You've been home all
these weeks, Mark, and haven't discovered that Lee was
Claire's lover. They used to meet at night in the shrubber-

ies. I knew but I didn't let on to Bertha. You can just imagine what a row there'd have been."

Mark was silent. Of course. He had seen them himself, and had mistaken the woman for one of the maids. What a crew, he thought bitterly. Mrs. Trant laid a hand on his arm.

"Don't blame her too much."

"I'm not blaming her," he said with unexpected gentleness. "Did she leave any message for me, Nannie? I'd better go into the town and ask old Ramsay to do what he can for her."

"You'll have a bit of dinner first, Master Mark. You look fair worn out."

"All right." Mark made an effort as the study door opened, and smiled at his half brother. "Here's old George wanting his grub."

George looked round at them all doubtfully. It was evident that he had heard their raised voices and was vaguely aware that there was something amiss.

"Where's Bertha?" he said.

It was the first time he had asked for her.

No one answered him, but Mark took his arm, and they went into the dining-room together.

CHAPTER XXII
LEGAL AID

THE FIRM of solicitors who had charge of the Armour estate were Ramsay, Johnstone, Synett and Ramsay. Old Mr. Ramsay had drawn up John Armour's will, under protest, and he had seen its conditions carried out. He bowed to Mark, when the young man was shown into his room, without offering his hand. He was the highly respected senior partner of a highly respectable firm and the idea of being involved in a sensational murder trial was very distasteful to him.

Mark had been prepared for a chilly reception. He sat on the chair indicated and stated his business in the fewest possible words. "My sister Claire has been arrested. I've come to ask you to act for her."

Mr. Ramsay was startled and showed it. "Your sister, Claire! Good God!" He checked himself. He had been about to say, "I thought it would be you." He adjusted his glasses and looked at Mark more closely. He was shocked at what he saw, the traces of suffering and of sleepless-ness. "My dear sir," he exclaimed involuntarily, "you've been ill!"

"No. I'm all right. I've been worried, naturally. Will you do what you can for Claire, Mr. Ramsay?" The lawyer cleared his throat nervously. "What is the charge?"

"I don't know exactly. I was out when the police came. I gathered that it had something to do with the death of Emily Watts."

"Dear me! I understood that her death was due to nat-ural causes. She failed to appear at the adjourned inquest, didn't she? A material witness. H'm. Your sister went to see her possibly? She wouldn't know that that was inad-visable. One may be accused of tampering or attempting to tamper with the evidence. You're quite sure that there's no mistake? She is actually under arrest? I think I'd better ring up the police and see what they have to say." He picked up his receiver. The one-sided conversation that followed conveyed nothing fresh to Mark beyond the main fact that it had a depressing effect on the lawyer. After it ceased there was a pregnant pause.

"I'm sorry," said Mr. Ramsay at last. "It's more serious than I anticipated. I suggested bail, but it seems that she is being held on a—on a capital charge—or nearly. Of being privy to the attempted murder of Emily Watts. Apparently the police are in possession of some fresh evidence. Your sister and Lee, the gardener, are to be brought before the local Bench of Magistrates to-morrow." He hesitated. "The police wouldn't have done this, Mr. Armour, if they hadn't something to go upon. I gathered that Lee admits going to the house on Marine Parade, where Emily Watts was staying, on the night of her death, and apparently they had words. And it seems there is some evidence that your sister Claire was there also." Mr. Ramsay cleared his throat. "Has this man Lee been in your service long?"

"About eighteen months, I think."

"Were you aware that—that he was on unusually friendly terms with your youngest sister?"

"No. Winnie told me just now."

"Your sister Bertha would not have countenanced anything of that sort?"

"Good Heavens, no! She'd have raised hell if she'd found out."

"Yes. Yes, no doubt. She was strict, eh. Dear me! It's very unfortunate. We must face facts, Mr. Armour, however unpleasant. Suppose they feared that she would—to use your own phrase—find out? It supplies a motive for—"

"You mean that they might have poisoned Bertha? That they will be accused of that?" Mark's face had lost its last vestige of colour. It had the pallor but not the peace of death. Mr. Ramsay got up hastily and produced a bottle of brandy and a glass from a corner cupboard.

"This has been a shock, eh?" he said not unkindly. "Drink this. I'll open the window for a moment. It's rather close in here. Now sit quietly for a minute. Plenty of time."

He busied himself with some papers on his desk, giving his client an opportunity to regain his self-control before he resumed.

"Now about the night before last. The police seem to think she went to this house on Marine Parade. Emily Watts visited the police station at about nine, so it would be later than that. If you could prove that she was at home all that evening it might be helpful—but for God's sake don't involve yourself in well-meant lies, Mr. Armour. That would do more harm than good in the end."

"I can't prove anything," said Mark. "We had supper together, the four of us, about seven. Afterwards I saw my brother George to bed. My sisters went to their rooms. At least I imagine so. We're not a sociable family, Mr. Ramsay. We're not in the habit of sitting together. I suppose we were all dreading the coming ordeal before the Coroner, being pointed out and stared at."

"Naturally," said the lawyer. "What did you do?"

Mark shrugged his shoulders. "Nothing to be proud of. I took half a bottle of whisky up to my room and finished it. I haven't been able to sleep, if that's any excuse for making a beast of myself. I've plenty of failings, but too much drink hasn't been one of them hitherto. I'd have tried some kind of dope, but no chemist here would supply me with anything lethal now. We shall have to change our name to Borgia. More suitable, what!"

He began to laugh. The lawyer laid a hand on his arm. "Stop that, Armour. Pull yourself together. This is a terrible business and a great deal depends on you. I will go round to the station at once and see your sister. I shall suggest that she instructs me to brief counsel. Mellor is a good man. Young and keen. He would do his best. I should advise you to go home and await events. I will keep you informed of what is being done."

"Go home and wait while the legal machinery is set in motion that will end in hanging Claire."

"No, no, no! We mustn't take a gloomy view. Isn't it possible that Lee is the—excuse my plain speaking—the sole culprit? Your sister may be able to clear herself before this goes any further. Let me see. You're not on the telephone at the White House?"

"No."

"Then I suggest that you wait here while I go over to the station and make sure that your mountain isn't a mole hill."

"Thank you," said Mark. "I'll do that. I'd like to know for certain before I go back. My half brother and sister are a great responsibility, Mr. Ramsay. I was wondering if it would be possible to have George boarded with a doctor who takes slight mental cases. He's perfectly harmless, poor chap, but he has to be looked after as though he were a small child. He's fond of Claire and I'm afraid he'll miss her, and if I—if I wasn't there either I don't know what would happen. One can't rely on Winnie. She only thinks about herself. She's weak in the head, too, of course, but not bad enough to be certified."

"It's a difficult position for you," agreed the lawyer. "As a matter of fact I happen to know that Doctor Marlow, at

Parminster, takes patients, just two or three, who are not quite normal. I'll get in touch with him if you like."

"Could you ring him up now? I'd like to feel George was being properly looked after. This doctor would be kind to him?"

"Oh, you needn't worry about that. Marlow is an excellent fellow. I know him well. I'll ring up and find out if he's in."

He took down his receiver and gave the doctor's number.

The ensuing conversation was brief but satisfactory. "He'll motor over to fetch him this evening between five and six if that will suit you? Good."

"They'll let him have his scrap albums and do his cutting out?" said Mark anxiously. "It's his only amusement, except a bit of gardening."

The lawyer reassured him. "Now I'll be off to see your sister. I'll ring up the office from there and my clerk will give you my message." He opened the outer door. "Benson, give Mr. Armour *The Times* to look at. He will be waiting here until I ring up."

Mark, left alone, tried to read the paper, but found himself unable to concentrate his attention on the printed page. He was feeling as he had felt years ago when he crouched in a muddy trench in Flanders waiting for the signal to go over the top. He had been afraid then, but he had had companions, and there had been some comfort in that. Ramsay, of course, didn't understand. It would not be enough to get Claire off and leave Lee to his fate. The scapegoat. He remembered a picture he had seen somewhere of the poor, dying brute stumbling along a stony track into the desert.

A dusty, shambling sort of exit. Why not a final flourish? Not poison. There had been too much of that.

The telephone bell rang in the managing clerk's room and Mark stiffened to attention. After a brief interval Benson came in to him.

"Mr. Ramsay has just rung up, sir. He asks me to tell you that he has seen Miss Armour and has had a talk with Superintendent Brisling. He is sorry to say that the matter appears to be very serious and that he fears that the question of bail will not be considered in either case."

"I see," said Mark. He had had to moisten his lips before he could utter. Benson glanced at him and averted his eyes quickly.

"Poor devil!" he thought.

"You'll probably get an official notice to appear to-morrow morning, Mr. Armour," he said. "Mr. Ramsay gathered that you would be called as a witness."

"To-morrow? All right." Mark reached for his hat. "Thank you," he said, and held out his hand. Benson, as he took it, was aware of his charm.

"I can't help feeling sorry for him," he told his fellow clerk when Mark had gone. "It isn't only his extraordinary good looks. They attract the women but cut no ice with me. It's a sort of look in his eyes that I've seen in those of a lost dog."

"You're too soft-hearted," said the other. "You know they're saying the chap's been a professional gigolo for years. That sort of appeal is a part of his technique, as purely mechanical as a dancer's fixed smile. That sister of his is probably not the first old lady he's bumped off. If I were the boss I'd wash my hands of all this Armour business and let them betake themselves to some other firm. It won't do us much good to be mixed up in their affairs."

Benson shook his head. "Too late for that now." He lowered his voice. "This mustn't go any further. I gathered from what Mr. Ramsay said just now over the 'phone that Bertha Armour was poisoned by her younger sister Claire, with the assistance of the gardener."

The other whistled. "You don't say so! Well, I'm damned! *Cave!* Here's the boss!"

They both became absorbed in their writing as Mr. Ramsay passed through the room.

CHAPTER XXIII
THE CAP—AND THE WINDMILL

THE FATES, for the most part, work unseen, but there are moments when they can almost be descried, like clouds forming in a sky of storm, brooding, implacable, about to complete some pattern on their tremendous loom. Mark, trudging home in the gathering dusk, was vaguely aware of the immortal shuttle flashing in and out of the web of his life.

A man standing at the gate of Mrs. Trant's cottage called to him as he was about to pass.

"Mr. Armour, isn't it?"

Mark saw that it was Dr. Cardew. He stiffened, for he had come to regard the doctor as an enemy. If Cardew was going to complain about Winnie again he would have to tell him that he had no control over her.

"I've some bad news for you, Mr. Armour. Mrs. Trant has met with an accident. Don't be too alarmed,"—he added, for Mark had caught at the gate post to steady himself. "She's working for you, isn't she? She was hurrying home, she tells me, to feed her chickens, and she slipped and fell on this brick path leading up to her door. Fortunately a passing milkman heard her cry out and fetched me. Her leg is broken and she'll have to be taken to the hospital and stay there a few weeks. I've sent for the ambulance and am expecting it at any moment now. I had promised her I would let you know."

"Thanks," said Mark curtly. "I'll go in and see her."

He found the old woman lying on the sofa in the kitchen clutching the paper parcel of clothing that a neighbour had got ready for her and crying silently. She was pathetically pleased to see him.

"Oh, Master Mark, dearie, that this should have happened just now! I was planning to go back to get your tea when I'd fed my fowls, and to shut up the cottage, and stay along with you till things were more settled. What will you do now without Miss Claire, with meals to get and all, and that Winnie mooning about—with her finery and trash?"

He stooped to kiss her wrinkled cheek. "Don't you worry, Nannie. You've done your best for us. We'll manage somehow. I've found a home for George in a doctor's house in Parminster. He's going to be fetched away this evening."

He was holding her hand, and he felt the work-worn fingers trembling in his grasp. "What about Claire?" she whispered. "Will she have to spend a night in a police cell? I can't bear to think of it."

"She'll be out to-morrow, Nannie. I promise you."

"You can't make them let her go, dearie."

"I think I can," he said. "Hush—here's the ambulance. Is there anything I can do for you?"

"Lock up and keep the key, dearie. My neighbour's going to look after the fowls. She'll get the eggs so there's no obligation. I'll be back as soon as I can."

He followed the two stretcher bearers with their load to the waiting ambulance and saw it start before he went on. Cardew was going with her and the two men did not exchange another word. Mark crossed the railway bridge with a glance at the signals at the bend. The 4.50 was due. He had not much time to prepare George for his departure. "If only he goes quietly!" he thought anxiously. The white gate clanged behind him. He limped up the drive between the dark dank walls of dripping laurels and entered the house. Perhaps Winnie would help to pack her brother's clothes. In any case she would have to be told that he was going.

Mark knocked at her bedroom door.

"It's me, Winnie. I want to speak to you."

"All right." To his relief she sounded cheerful. She came out on to the landing with a hat partly trimmed in her hand. "What is it? Heavens! Mark, you do look tired!"

"I am rather. Will you get the tea, Winnie, or shall I? We've got to wait on ourselves now. Mrs. Trant's had a fall and has been taken to the hospital."

"How tiresome! We shall have to get somebody else. In a way I shan't mind. I know you and Claire are fond of her and that she was your nurse years ago and all that, but I think she's inclined to be rather familiar and presuming. I do like servants to keep their places. Do get the tea if you know how, Mark. I want to finish this hat."

"You'll have time for the hat later," he said. "That isn't all. I've arranged for George to go and stay in a doctor's family at Parminster for the present. They're coming to fetch him. We shall have to pack his clothes."

"A doctor! How thrilling! Is he young? Is he a friend of Ian's?"

"Who's Ian?"

"Doctor Cardew. We're engaged, you know, but it's a secret for the present. Until all this blows over."

"Oh!" Mark felt unequal to making any comment. "We've got to see about George now," he said, trying not to sound impatient. "I'm going up to the loft to find something to put his clothes into. I'll shove his stuff in and break the news to him if you'll get the tea. Will you do that?"

"Oh, very well," she said ungraciously, "if I must."

He found among the lumber of thirty years an old portmanteau that had belonged to his father, and filled it with George's scanty wardrobe. Then he went down to the study. The snipping of George's scissors ceased as he entered, and the dim eyes in the mild bearded face met his trustfully. Mark was conscious of a pang of something like remorse. He was trying to do his best for George, but the White House was his home. Would he be happy elsewhere?

"Look here, George, old chap, I'm going to make a nice parcel of that album you're working on and that pile of picture papers and your paste pot and brush and scissors. You can carry it yourself if you like so that you'll be sure you've got it. You're going away on a little visit. There'll be a garden there, and lots to eat."

George gazed at him with no change of expression. "Will you be there?"

"No."

"Will Claire?"

"No."

"Then I won't go."

Mark was touched. That was as near as poor George was ever likely to get to expressing a preference. He sat down beside him.

"She'll be coming to see you, old chap. Won't you go to please us? It's a bit of a mess up here just now."

"All right."

"That's a good boy. Come into the dining-room—or we'll do up that parcel first, shall we?" He fetched brown paper and string and with some lumbering and tentative assistance from George, tied up the materials of his craft in a large bundle. They had just fastened the last knot when Winnie came to tell them she had made the tea.

The three of them sat down to a picnic meal in the dining-room. Mark cut bread and butter for his half-brother and spread it thickly with jam. He could not eat himself, but he drank two cups of tea. The car arrived before they had finished. Mark went to the door and found the doctor, a middle-aged man with a breezy manner, and a young woman in a nurse's uniform, on the step.

Doctor Marlow was brisk and business-like. "Your half-brother, isn't it? I hope he's ready. I'm rather pressed for time. Is that his luggage? Give me a hand with it and we'll put it on the car. I've a luggage carrier. That's right. Now, where is he?"

Mark went back to the dining-room.

"Come along, George, old chap," he said huskily. George rose obediently and turned to pick up his parcel. They went into the hall together.

"This is my brother, Doctor. He'll be allowed to do his cutting out?"

"Yes, yes," the doctor was reassuring. The nurse said nothing, but she took George's arm and led him out. Mark dug his nails into his palms. George. He had not realised how fond he was of George until he saw that shambling figure being taken down the steps to the car.

Winnie had come out of the dining-room and was talking in her high, affected company voice to the doctor, who answered briefly, and was obviously anxious to get away. Mark went down to the car. The nurse had got in and was sitting beside George, who had refused to be parted from his parcel and was holding it on his knees.

"Good-bye, old man. God bless you."

George turned his head slowly. His round, childlike blue eyes were full of tears.

"Good-bye," he said.

The car started. Mark watched the red tail light disappear round the bend of the drive before he went back into the house. Winnie had vanished. He supposed she had gone upstairs again to finish trimming her hat. He returned to the dining-room and sat down before the fire to smoke a cigarette. Presently he threw the end into the grate and leaned forward, resting his elbows on his knees and his head in his hands. The house was deathly still. Not a sound but the ticking of the clocks. After a while he got up and went over to the old-fashioned bureau at which Bertha had sat over her housekeeping books. It needed no great effort of imagination to see her there now, a thick-set, ungainly figure in a mannish tweed coat and skirt of the clerical grey that was so unbecoming to her sallow complexion, adding up figures. If only he could recall an instance of her turning with a smile, a gleam, only one gleam of kindness on that hard face! An eye for an eye. That was Bertha's creed. Well, she was going to be satisfied.

He found a pen and some sheets of notepaper and sat down to write. The front door bell rang. "Damn!" said Mark. He did not want visitors now. Who could it be? The police again? Couldn't they leave him alone just a little longer?

He covered the few words he had written with a sheet of blotting paper before he went into the hall. The gas, turned low, flickered as he opened the door, letting in a gust of wind. The trees surrounding the house were tossing and creaking dismally in the rising gale. It was a dark night. Mark peered out, expecting to see the burly shape of Superintendent Brisling.

"Who is it?" He failed to keep the resentment he felt out of his voice.

The visitor moved forward uncertainly. He caught a glimpse of a red cap and a high storm collar framing a small pale face.

"My God! It's Lucy!"

"Oh, Mark—do you mind? I'll go away again if—"

He pulled her in and shut the door before he took her in his arms. For several minutes neither of them uttered another word. They clung together blindly, desperately, carried away on the tide of their passion. At last some sound overhead recalled Mark to the exigencies of their position. Winnie was upstairs, and the time was passing.

"Come in here," he said, and took her into the dining-room. "Oh, my darling, I thought I should never see you again."

"I wanted to come before, but I was a coward," she said, "And Uncle Geoffrey thought it might do you harm if I got mixed up in your troubles. But I've wanted you so! I couldn't stick it any longer. Oh, Mark, how dreadfully ill and worn you look!"

He sat down in the big armchair by the fire and drew her on to his knees. "Don't look at me, Lucy. Kiss me. You don't believe I'm a murderer?"

"No. Of course not." He felt her hesitation. "Is it true that they've arrested your younger sister?"

"Yes."

"Oh, Mark! Is it possible that she did it?"

"No. They'll let her go in the morning." He groaned. What would she be thinking of him to-morrow? Could he carry out his purpose now that he knew that she loved him still? But what other road was there?

"Lucy, do your people know about us?"

"I haven't dared tell Daddie or Aunt Mary, but Geoffrey guessed I was unhappy and made me confide in him. He's been very decent, Mark, and he's been trying to help you. He's done police work himself in the East and he's been making enquiries, and he's hired a private detective who's supposed to be frightfully clever. Mark"—she looked at him anxiously—"you don't mind?"

For the first time she was conscious of a doubt. Why didn't he answer. Suppose that, after all, he was guilty of that awful crime? She slipped from his arms and he made no effort to detain her. She stood, supporting herself with one hand by the mantelpiece, and staring down at the tragic, huddled figure in the deep armchair. Her lover— and a murderer? Why didn't he stand up too and face the world and defy it? Was it that he couldn't? She was trembling, sick with horror. "Do you mind?" she repeated, and now her voice was hard.

"Mind? I'm afraid I do. Your Uncle may have meant kindly, but his interference may do infinite harm. Some things are better left alone. I know what has to be done now to clear up the mess, and I'm going to do it. Tell him that, will you, and ask him to stop."

"Very well," she said faintly. "I—I think I'll go now." She stooped to pick up her red cap that had fallen off, and moved towards the door. Mark turned his head to watch her go. Should he call her back? He was sorely tempted. Her faith in him, her love, had been the one thing left to him. He knew her impulsive generosity, her divine imprudence. If he called she would come. He bit his lips hard. Let her go thinking the worst. It was the one thing he could do to repair the wrong he had done her. He would hear her steps crossing the hall, the closing of the front door. Then silence and the last things. But instead, startling them both, came the clanging of the door bell.

Lucy stopped short and Mark was beside her in a moment.

"You must not be found here. Will you go out by the window while I answer the door? Go round the house, turning to the left when you get outside, and you'll find your way to the drive." He knew he should have stopped there, but his resolution failed him. "God bless you, my darling," he said, and lifted her hand to his lips.

She turned to him instantly, with a pitiful eagerness. "Mark, for God's sake, say you didn't do it! Tell me the truth! I can bear anything else. Even if—if we never meet again."

"I swear!" he said, "but no one else will believe." There was no time for more. The bell was ringing again. He unlatched the window for her and the wind blowing in stirred the heavy curtains. "Quick!" he said. Their lips met in a hurried kiss.

CHAPTER XXIV
AN S.O.S.

MARK OPENED the front door and the man standing outside stepped past him into the hall. He was a middle-aged man, lean and brown, with close-cropped grey hair, and his face was vaguely familiar.

"My name is Raynham," he said, "I'm staying at Dennyford with my brother-in-law, Colonel Rivers."

Mark said nothing. He wanted to gain time. Lucy must be half way down the drive by now, he thought. So this was her Uncle Geoffrey. He remembered that she had said that her uncle knew everything. Yes, and he was making enquiries that might be well meant but were likely to prove disastrous. He would have to be stopped somehow.

"I'm afraid I must seem intrusive," said Raynham, "but I've a good reason for coming as I think you'll agree when I explain. Of course I may have jumped to a wrong conclusion."

"Will you come in here?" said Mark hesitatingly. He glanced about him nervously as he led the way into the dining-room. Had Lucy left anything behind her? Apparently not. He detected a faint scent of violets, but probably it was too slight to be noticed by any sense less acute than a lover's.

"Sit down, won't you. Will you have a drink?" Some devil of perversity made him add, "I won't put any arsenic in it."

"Thanks," said Raynham, deliberately, "I'm not afraid of that. A whisky and soda if you've got that handy. And have one yourself. I fancy you need it."

"Are you a doctor?"

"No. But I've done a bit of psycho-analysis in the course of my career and I can generally tell when a man's had about as much worry as he can stand. That's your case, isn't it?"

"I won't say you're wrong. Oh, damn, I've spilt some."

He brought over the two glasses. Raynham, who was still standing, took his with a grave inclination of his head, and drank without hesitation.

"Thank you," said Mark, and drank also.

They both sat down and Raynham passed the younger man his cigarette-case.

"You haven't a wireless?" he said abruptly.

"No."

"Well, I'd better clear the ground a bit before I tell you what has brought me here, like the Erl König, *durch Nacht und Wind*. I hold a watching brief in this case for an interested party, Armour. The mother of Lucy Rivers was my only sister, and I loved her very dearly. I want her child to be happy. That's rather a large order in this world, but at any rate I want her to avoid being fearfully unhappy. When I came here, after an absence of several years abroad, I found her grown into a charming girl, but —well, the happiness was to seek. I gained her confidence and heard about you."

"You can't blame me more than I blame myself," said Mark. "I—we drifted into it. It's the one good thing I've ever had. I don't ask you to forgive me. Be kind to her. Take her away from here and she may forget in time."

"If your innocence of this crime can be proved, Armour, wouldn't it be possible for you to start again in one of the colonies? I think I could help you. I happen to be part owner of a tea plantation in Ceylon, for instance. The manager is leaving—but we can talk of that later."

"You are very kind," said Mark, "but I'm afraid my innocence won't be proved."

"Well—I won't press that now," said Raynham. "You will be wondering why I came out here tonight. I asked you just now if you had the wireless. The Rivers have a portable. They were all out this afternoon and I had my tea alone in the drawing-room and switched on the radio afterwards to get some distraction—I need not tell you that I have been troubled about my niece. The announcer from the London station prefaced the news with an S.O.S. The Commissioner of Police was anxious to trace the friends or relations of a woman who was knocked down by a taxicab outside Charing Cross station on the morning of the 24th of October as she was attempting to board a bus to Victoria. She was removed to Charing Cross Hospital where she is lying dangerously ill. There was a fog at the time and a crowd collected, and it appears that the suit-case she was carrying and her handbag were stolen. She has not been identified, but she is believed to be a Frenchwoman—"

Mark half rose from his chair and sank back again. Raynham was watching him closely without seeming to do so.

"A broadcast description followed. Age about fifty-five. Medium height and inclined to be stout. Black hair and eyes and must have been very beautiful when younger. Poorly dressed in black. This woman has been asking repeatedly for her children but is unable or unwilling to give their names. Her condition is hopeless and she is sinking rapidly."

Mark made a restless movement. "What makes you think—"

"I can't tell you that. As I listened it occurred to me that your mother was French. It's a million to one chance— unless you happen to be aware that she was in London at that date and that she might be on her way to catch the boat train."

There was a pause before the younger man replied. "You are in with the police," he said. "How am I to know that this isn't a trap?"

"I give you my word," said Raynham earnestly. "My connection with this case isn't an official one, though I have discussed it with Brisling. I switched off the wireless and came straight here. I'll drive you up to Town now if you like, Armour, and, if we are mistaken, I'll bring you back again in time for breakfast. If this woman is a stranger you will have lost nothing."

"It's good of you," said Mark. "I'll accept your offer. I— it's horribly difficult to decide. More difficult than you re-alise," he added feverishly.

"I've got my car in the road."

"I must just run up and tell Winnie I shall be away for the night. She won't like being left alone, but it can't be helped."

Raynham waited for him in the hall. Mark was not gone long.

"It's all right," he said briefly. "She didn't seem to mind."

It was pitch dark in the drive and silent but for the crunching of the loose gravel under their feet and the steady drip drip of the rain on the laurels. Raynham had stopped the engine of his car. He climbed into the driver's seat and Mark got in beside him. Raynham put in the clutch. They had travelled a couple of miles before he spoke.

"Was that somebody coming up to your gate as we started?"

"I didn't notice."

"I saw something move. It occurred to me that it might be a policeman."

"It might have been the postman. He sometimes comes about seven on the last round. We don't get many letters, but they might send the summons to attend the inquest on Emily by post."

"Hell!" said Raynham. He swerved to avoid a lorry. "I'd forgotten that. We shall have to get back for that. I can't account for Emily," he said thoughtfully.

Mark did not ask him what he meant. He was too tired for consecutive thought, and after a while he slept. They passed through Horsham. Raynham accelerated, and the car roared through the darkness. The hedgerows streamed by, every twig and blade of grass flashing out in the white glare of the headlights for a fraction of time to sink back again into the peaceful obscurity of the November night when they had passed.

Mark was awakened by a sudden grinding of brakes. The car had stopped by the roadside.

"A skid?" he began.

"No," said Raynham grimly. "A stowaway." He switched on the light inside the car and turned to look at the intruder.

"My God! It's Lucy! How did you get here, child!"

"Never mind that, Uncle Geoff darling. I'll explain later. I'm here, and you can't put me out miles from home."

"I suppose not. Did you know she was there, Armour?"

"No."

Lucy was still very pale, but her eyes were bright. "Hadn't you better drive on?" she suggested. "We're wasting time. May Mark sit at the back with me?"

"No, he may not," growled Raynham. "Your father is bound to hear of this, Lucy. I'll have to ring him up from the next A.A. box."

"You can tell him you're taking me up to London to a show."

"I'm not going to tell him any lies."

"Well—up to London. That's true, anyway," said Lucy unabashed.

"I don't know what young women are coming to."

"They're just the same as they always were, Geoffrey." Her voice changed, losing the rather forced note of gay defiance. "Let Mark sit with me," she pleaded. "He's been so unhappy and so have I. Mark, you want to, don't you?"

"Lucy," he said huskily, "your uncle is being extraordinarily good to me. He's right. We must play the game."

"And that's that, my dear," said her uncle. He drove on. After a while he fancied he heard her sobbing, but he did not turn his head.

Lucy dried her eyes presently and hunted in her handbag for her powder puff and mirror. She was very conscious of Mark's rigid back and shoulders, set as if on parade. She must not make things worse for him. They were bad enough. On the spur of the moment she had waited, hidden behind the window curtains of the dining-room, instead of taking the opportunity afforded her of leaving the house.

The rest had followed naturally. She had slipped out when the two men quitted the room, and while Mark went upstairs to speak to Winnie she had run down the drive and got into the back of her uncle's car. She did not regret her action. "I've been skulking long enough," she told herself. She meant to come out now openly on Mark's side. They stopped at Dorking, and Raynham went into the post office to telephone to Colonel Rivers. While he was gone his two passengers exchanged a few hurried words.

"Mark, you're not angry with me for coming?"

"My darling, no! But I'm worried. It may mean trouble for you later. Promise me you'll do what Raynham tells you. He'll look after you."

"Mark, do you really think this poor woman you're going to see may be your mother?"

"It is possible."

Lucy sat back as Raynham climbed into the driver's seat.

"It's a good thing I rang up," he said. "They were beginning to get the wind up."

"What did you tell daddie?"

"I told him I was taking you up to Town and that we should be home very late or put up at an hotel. He assumed that I was taking you to a theatre, and I didn't undeceive him. Are you warm enough, Lucy?"

Something in his tone told her that she was forgiven. She leaned forward. "Yes, dear. Thank you so much. Thank you for everything."

"That's all right," he said gruffly. "Look out. Don't distract the driver's attention. We shall land in a ditch."

Chapter XXV
"NOT THAT—"

THE HOUSE-SURGEON stared hard at Mark. "You have a missing relative? Your mother? There's a strong likeness. Remarkable. You heard the wireless appeal?"

Raynham answered for him. "Yes. Is there any hope?"

The house-surgeon shook his head. "She was unconscious until a few hours ago. We operated for the removal of a splinter of bone pressing on the brain. She has been conscious since and calling for her children. Will you come with me, Mr.—"

"Armour."

"Lucy and I will go round to my flat. It's not two minutes' walk from here," said Raynham.

"I'd rather you came with me, sir," said Mark. "I'd like you to know if—if she has anything to say."

"Very well. You wait here, then, Lucy."

"If her suit-case and handbag hadn't been stolen we could have communicated with her family," said the doctor. "She must have had papers of some kind. Most unfortunate. She said something about a daughter."

"I'm afraid her daughter couldn't be here in time if she's—"

"She's on the danger list. I don't think she can live through the night."

They followed their guide down a long white corridor smelling faintly of ether and carbolic into the small bare room where a nurse rose to receive them. She, too, looked hard at Mark and moved instinctively to make way for him to stand by the narrow iron bed on which the patient lay.

The huge, dark eyes deep sunken in the grey face on the pillow had been fixed unwinkingly on the ceiling. They turned now and brightened. The pale lips moved. "Mark—*mon cher*. I have met with a little accident—you have heard."

He knelt by the bedside. "Mother darling. How did it happen?"

"I had taken the car in which I drove down to see you back to the garage and fetched my bag from my lodgings. I was hurrying to catch the boat train at Victoria. Crossing the road—I do not remember any more. *Je suis brisée*—I am afraid—it is finished."

"Mother"—tears ran down his cheeks. "Oh, why did you—"

"What?" she said feebly. "Don't cry, *mon petit*. How goes it at home? That Bertha—is she as insupportable as ever?"

She turned her head a little as he did not reply. "What is the matter, Mark? Why do you look at me like that? Has anything happened?"

The doctor had left them and the nurse had withdrawn to the other side of the room. Only Raynham remained just outside the little circle of light cast by the shaded lamp.

"Don't you remember?" said Mark gently. "Bertha is dead."

"Dead? But how sudden. Was she ill? You never told me."

"Mother—" Mark's voice was suddenly urgent, "didn't you go into Bertha's room that night you came down to see me? Didn't you go in and find her asleep and—and put something in her glass of milk?"

"I? Never. You were out and I waited in your room until you came in. The rest you know. I saw no one else—not even Claire."

"Oh!" he gasped, "forgive me! All this time I thought—she's been poisoned—and I thought—"

"Doucement," she murmured. "Bertha, *hein*? She hated me always, and I her. But to kill—no—many sins in my life, but not that. *C'est drôle, quand meme"*—she began to laugh and began to cough terribly, struggling for breath. The nurse hurried over to the bedside and leaned over her, wiping blood from her lips with a pad of cotton wool.

Raynham went into the corridor. He met the house-surgeon leaving another ward and spoke to him before he rejoined Lucy in the waiting-room.

"I'm going to take you to my flat. It's just round the corner from here. It will be better. Armour will join us later. I've arranged that."

"Is it his mother?" she asked.

"Yes. And she's dying."

"Oh, poor Mark."

He refused to say anything more until they had had some food and a cup of coffee which he made himself over a spirit lamp, and were comfortably established in the sitting-room of his bachelor flat. He looked at his watch before he lit his cigarette.

"Twenty-five minutes past ten. I wonder if I ought to ring up the superintendent. If he finds out that Armour left the White House in a car he may get worried."

"Let him!" said Lucy vigorously. "Interfering beast! Geoffrey, I can't help putting two and two together. Mrs. Armour was run over the very morning that Bertha Armour died. Was it just a coincidence?"

"Yes," he said, "I think so. A damnably unlucky one for her son. I can tell you more or less what happened. Mrs. Armour, of course, couldn't show her face at the White House while her step-daughter was mistress there. She had heard of her son's accident and that he was living at home with the others. She was over in England for a few days and she couldn't resist running down on the chance of seeing him. She drove herself down in a hired car which she left a little way up the road, and entered the house by the unlatched study window, and crept up the back stairs to Mark's bedroom. It was past midnight and the household had retired to rest, but Mark was not there."

"We were on the beach that night," said Lucy.

"Quite," said her uncle drily. "Now some of this is deduction, but I don't think I'm far out. When the young man came in Mrs. Armour had given him up and was just coming down the back stairs. They had a brief and hurried colloquy. He may or may not have gone down to the waiting car with her. Then he returned to the house and went to bed and to sleep. You can imagine, Lucy, what awful suspicion entered his mind when he learned that Bertha had been poisoned by arsenic administered by some unknown hand during that night. The motive was obvious—to free her children from the domination of their half-sister. Probably he assumed that his mother had gone back to France. In any case, I think he was prepared to go to almost any length to save her. He has always been devoted to his mother. Do you know anything of the past history of the Armours?"

"I've heard that Mrs. Armour ran away with the French Master of a preparatory school on the Marine Parade."

"Yes. Mrs. Trant, who was cook at the White House then, told me all about it. Mark was about thirteen then. Three years later she wrote to her husband begging him to send her a little money. Her lover was dead and she was down and out in Paris. The old man told Mark and his sister, adding that he hadn't the slightest intention of helping her and that she might starve for all he cared. He tore up her letter. Mark got the pieces from the waste paper basket and discovered her address. He had not a penny of his own. He forged his father's name on a cheque. The manager of the local bank spotted it. His father turned him out—"

"Oh, that was why!" cried Lucy. "I think that was splendid!"

"Well, that's ancient history," said Raynham. "She's dying now but conscious and apparently in full possession of her mental faculties—and she never went near Bertha that night, and didn't know of her death. He practically told her what he had suspected, and she denied it. I, for one, am disposed to believe her."

Lucy gazed at him. "Then who did that—that awful thing?"

"That's still an open question," said Raynham. "You see this will lift a terrible weight from Armour's mind, but it won't clear him. Even if she lived long enough to make a statement before witnesses and sign it."

"Wouldn't that be any use?"

"None. If he did it he may have dropped the stuff in the milk earlier in the evening, before he went out to meet you."

"Well, the police have arrested Claire," said Lucy. "It's all over Dennyford. I heard it this afternoon at the hairdresser's. It will still be ghastly for Mark, naturally."

Raynham shook his head. "Glide thinks the local police have gone off on a false scent. And yet he himself supplied the most damning bit of evidence against her. He's a queer chap."

"What was it?"

He hesitated. "I ought not to tell you. It was a footprint. You'll hear all about that soon enough. Look here, child, we may be here most of the night. Lie down on that settee and try to sleep." He fetched an eiderdown from his bed and wrapped her up in it. "You're tired out."

She looked up at him wistfully. "You're good to me, Geoffrey. And you do believe that Mark is innocent, don't you? You must."

"My dear—" He dared not tell her that in spite of his profound pity for Mark Armour he was not entirely convinced that he had not, on that fatal night, yielded to a terrible temptation. That Lucy loved him was no proof. Murderers were often loved; they were often very attractive to women. "Try to sleep," he repeated.

Her lips trembled, but she closed her eyes obediently.

Raynham went to the window and drew the curtain. The London night was an Aladdin's cave of jewels. Rubies, emeralds, flashed on invisible trees. The lights of the Embankment were like a string of gold beads. The siren of a steamer going down with the tide wailed like a lost soul. A lost soul. Raynham shuddered. Who killed Bertha Armour? That question was still unanswered. He had assumed to Lucy that Mark had suspected his mother. But had he? He might have had the best of all reasons for knowing her to be guiltless. That little scene at her bedside might have been played for his, Raynham's, benefit. A fluent and resourceful liar.

And yet—didn't the circumstances of the second death absolve him and furnish convincing proof of Claire Armour's guilt? Claire and the gardener. Wouldn't the arsenic found in Emily Watts' cup of cocoa suffice to hang them both, even though she had died of heart failure? If only they had thought to throw the stuff away and rinse the cup in the sink before they left her! "But of course they were badly rattled," he thought, "and murderers always make one mistake."

Lucy was asleep. He could hear her soft even breathing. "A good thing," he told himself. "She'll have to face her father to-morrow. To-morrow. My God!" He lit another cigarette and sat, watching the lights. Eleven o'clock. Twelve.

CHAPTER XXVI
THIS FREEDOM

WINNIE TURNED OVER the bunches of more or less faded artificial flowers and lengths of ribbon that she had hoarded for years in a cardboard box under her bed. She was trying to retrim a mauve felt shape in the style of a French model she had seen in the window of Ellis and Stroud, in the High Street. Just a twist of velvet round the crown and a bunch of Parma violets to hide an accidental smear of ink on the brim.

She was incapable of thinking much or clearly about other people's affairs, but recent events were sufficiently out of the usual course to attract even her attention, and she was reviewing the situation as she worked. It was queer, she felt, to be alone in the house after all these years. She could do just as she liked at last. She smiled with satisfaction. Nobody to say "Winnie, don't do that!" or "Winnie, I'm sorry to hear"—or—"Winifred, I am ashamed." She had not thought when Bertha died that the others would be going too. Like an avalanche. You dislodge one stone in your path and the whole mountain side goes crashing down into the abyss. No. That was stupid. It was nothing like that. George was gone to a place where they would take great care of him. Claire. It was Claire's own fault for letting Lee make love to her. Mark would be coming back. She would not be free for long, after all. Not that Mark ordered her about as Bertha had done. Bertha had screamed at her that last time and said horribly cruel things. Winnie's delicate pink and white face quivered at the recollection of her elder sister's attempts to keep her in order. "I mustn't get morbid!" she said aloud.

The hat was finished. She tried it on before her glass. "It suits me," she murmured and moved the candles to get a different light. The little face with the weak chin and the wild, light eyes peeped coyly back at her.

Ian Cardew. She wrote every day. He could not say that she was not faithful. She gave of her best. He didn't answer, but that was because he had to be so very careful, being a professional man. When all the fuss was over her money would buy him a practice in another part of England. "We'll have two children," she thought. "A boy and a girl. Or perhaps three."

The clock on the landing struck eight. It was still quite early. She had the whole evening before her and she was alone in the house and safe from comment or criticism. Why shouldn't she slip out for an hour and pay Ian a surprise visit? The last of the out-patients would have gone and no one need know. Her brain only retained a very vague and confused recollection of former rebuffs and humiliations. She could always explain those to her satisfaction as the painful impression made on her at the time faded. She put on her coat and hunted in her drawers for a pale pink scarf to wind round her neck. One end was torn but it wouldn't show if she tucked, it in.

It was a dark night and she met no one on the road. A light shone dimly through the fanlight over the doctor's door. Cardew came himself in answer to her ring at the bell. For some days now she had ceased to haunt the terrace and he was taken by surprise. He had been busy in his dispensary making up medicines, for the Armour case had had the unexpected result of increasing the number of his patients. He was, therefore, in better spirits. His face fell as he saw the draggled figure on his doorstep, but his back was to the light and she missed the change of expression.

She gazed up at him adoringly. "Oh, Ian, I thought it would be all right to come just for a minute. Nobody knows. Mark's gone off somewhere. I'm quite on my own. Isn't it fun! You've had my letters?"

"Yes. I wish you wouldn't write to me, Miss Armour."

"Don't be so formal!" she reproached him. "Your housekeeper's deaf and the kitchen's a long way off. There's nobody in the surgery, is there?"

"No. But—"

"I know you've got to be careful!" she said, hugging her delusion. "It wouldn't do for you to be talked about. We've got to wait until they've stopped fussing. That's why I'd better come in, darling. Anybody passing in the road could see me standing at the door."

He bit his lip. He might have pushed her back and slammed the door in her face, but he lacked the necessary brutality. "Look here," he protested weakly, and then, "all right. Come in."

She slipped past him at once in her vague, sidelong fashion and drifted into the lit surgery. He closed the hall door and followed her, conscious of a sick reluctance. Her brother had done his best, but if he was away there was no chance of her being fetched home. What had become of the fellow? Had he bolted?

She was waiting for him in the middle of the room. He stayed near the door.

"I'm afraid there's some misunderstanding, Miss Armour," he began. "You speak as if we were old friends. We aren't. I don't make friends easily. I'm not what they call a woman's man. I don't want to be offensive but—but what you suggest is impossible."

Her rapt and blissful look faded a little. Her lower lip dropped like the lip of a disappointed child.

"Is it because they've arrested Claire? Because of the scandal about the gardener? It's horrid, I know, but she's only my half-sister, and we can go right away where no one will have heard."

"It's not that," he said. His harassed mind hunted for some further defence, and seized on a half-formed plan. "If I marry anybody, Miss Armour, it will be a girl I've known all my life. Her people lived next door to mine in Aberdeen."

"Oh!" She shrank as if he had struck her but still struggled on. "Has she any money?"

"No."

"Then she can't help you as I can. I thought you understood. I shall have a fourth share of everything, and it's all for you. You can buy a practice. You explain that to her and if she really cares for you she won't stand in your way."

A clean cut, he thought. No use messing about trying to be kind. He spoke slowly and distinctly. "I couldn't marry for money, Miss Armour. I couldn't marry a woman for whom I felt no affection. Please understand that this is absolutely my last word. I—I—" his firm front crumbled, "I simply can't stand it."

"Stand what?" Her strange light eyes were glazed like the eyes of a hare. He hated himself even while he allowed his deep underlying irritation to carry him away. A thing like this, soft, defenceless, that thrust itself upon one so that one had to strike blow after blow. "Intolerable!" he said aloud. "This persecution."

The truth filtered slowly into her mind. "Then you haven't wanted my letters?"

"No. I've burnt them unread. Miss Armour, why do you make me say these things!"

"I see." Blindly she turned towards the door. He passed out before her and opened the house door. To his relief she went by him without looking at him. He watched her go down the steps, holding to the rail, before he shut himself in and shot the bolts.

Winnie crept along the pavement to the end of the terrace. As she reached the road a little man who had been standing there waiting for her to come out of the doctor's house approached her.

"Miss Armour—"

"Who are you?"

"My name is Glide, and I have been engaged to solve the mystery of your sister's death. I'd like to ask you a few questions if I may."

She walked on and he walked beside her over the railway bridge. "He's quite civil," she thought. It was better than being alone. If only the fire in the dining-room hadn't gone out. She was chilled to the marrow. You couldn't think properly when you were so cold. Her teeth were chattering as they went up the drive. She did not invite Glide to come in, but he followed unasked, and, after one glance at her stricken face in the light of the hall lamp, assumed command.

"There!" he said when he had stirred the dining-room fire to a blaze and pushed the big armchair nearer. "Sit down and warm yourself." He looked towards the decanter of whisky and the two glasses on the side table. "Will you have some of that stuff? No? Well, I tell you what. I'll find my way down to the kitchen and make you a cup of tea. You've had a shock, haven't you? Just sit here and get warm."

She sat huddled over the fire, holding out her shaking hands to the flame. He was away some time. It was kind of him she thought dully. She would be glad of some tea. When he brought it she sipped it eagerly.

"Better now?" he said.

"Yes, thank you."

He sat down opposite her. "It's upset you, naturally," he said, "to think of your sister being hanged for murder."

Her empty cup clattered in the saucer as she set it down.

"What are you talking about! They've no evidence against Claire. It's absurd. They'll have to let her go. It won't do her any harm to spend a night or two in prison. She deserves to be punished for the way she's behaved. They went on about me, and all the time Claire was far worse. Lowering herself so. It's she who's disgraced the family."

"They've got evidence," he said. "It's all circumstantial, and they may be wrong, but they've got enough to convince a jury. Motive, opportunity, access to the poison—there was a half empty tin of weed killer in the potting shed. It might not have been enough if they hadn't tried to kill Emily to stop her from talking."

"But that's—Claire didn't—" she stopped herself.

"Well, it wouldn't be the first time the innocent has suffered for the guilty," said Glide, "but I'd rather be Abel than Cain, wouldn't you, Miss Armour?"

She made no answer.

Glide got up to go. There was something that bulged in his overcoat pocket. He had reached the door when he paused.

"By the way, you wear the same size in shoes as your sister, don't you? I thought so. Good night, Miss Armour."

CHAPTER XXVII
THE MORNING AFTER

IT WAS STILL DARK when Raynham stopped the car at the gate of the White House. Mark got out, moving stiffly, for he was numb with fatigue, and stood in the road.

"I don't know how to thank you for this, sir. But for you I should never have seen my mother again, and I should have gone on thinking that she—well, I think you've guessed what I thought."

"Yes."

Lucy had got out of the back of the car. "It will all come right, Mark."

For an instant they clung together.

"You'd better sit by me now, Lucy," said Raynham. "See you later, Armour."

She got in and they drove on.

"Now we come to the next bit," said Raynham grimly. "You'd better go straight up to bed and stay there."

"And leave you to face the music? I shall feel such a worm."

"I should think you'll feel a worm anyway," said Raynham, who was inclined to be crusty after a night up. "I don't want to be hard on you, Lucy, but this is going to be a nasty jar for your father and your aunt."

"I know," she murmured.

He was disarmed by her humility. "They'll get over it," he said. "It may even do them a bit of good in the end. They've got a trifle smug, I've noticed. People do in places like this"; he eyed the sleeping villa residences of Dennyford with a touch of contempt. They passed a policeman on his beat, who looked after them sharply, startled a stray cat, and saw at the far end of the Marine Parade, a milkman just starting on his round. The blinds at Simla were all down. Raynham brought the car well in to the kerb and turned off the engine, and they went up the garden path together.

"You haven't a latch-key, Lucy?"

"Good Heavens, no! Daddie wouldn't dream of trusting me with one. You'll have to ring and either he or Aunt Mary will come down. Our maids don't arrive until about seven."

Raynham gave the bell an impatient jerk and they waited. After an interval they heard the Colonel's heavy, shuffling steps and the door was opened.

He gazed at them in surprise. "What an extraordinary time to come home! I thought you were staying the night in Town. I hope you won't do this again, Raynham. It's very disturbing. Mary and I were quite anxious. And being brought down in my dressing-gown before six o'clock. You look like a ghost, Lucy. It's evident that theatre-going and late hours don't suit you."

"Run up to bed, Lucy," said her uncle. "She's very tired, Rivers."

"I daresay," growled the Colonel.

She slipped by him and ran up the stairs. He looked after her uneasily. "I say, there's nothing wrong, is there? You didn't have a smash? I've never seen her look like that."

"There is something," admitted Raynham. "It's got to be thrashed out. Better wait until after breakfast. We've been up all night. I need a bath and a shave."

"No," said the Colonel, "if it's anything concerning my little girl I'm not going to wait three hours to hear it. Come into the study, I'll put on the gas-fire."

"All right," said Raynham wearily. He had hoped for a short respite, but perhaps it was better to get the thing over at once. He would have to be careful though. Lucy's whole future might depend on the way he stated her case. He sat down and lit a cigarette.

"Mrs. Armour was knocked down by a motor in the Strand a fortnight ago and has been lying in Charing Cross Hospital ever since. Yesterday evening the B.B.C. broadcast an S.O.S. to her relatives, and I took Mark Armour up to London in my car. He was with his mother until she died between two and three o'clock. I brought him back at once as he will have to be present this morning when his sister is brought before the Bench on a charge of attempted murder."

The Colonel heard him with surprise mingled with indignation.

"And you took Lucy with you? Have you taken leave of your senses, Raynham? Mixing her up with that crew."

"John," said his brother-in-law, "I'm afraid what I have to say will be a shock to you. I want you to keep two facts in mind. The first is that Lucy's a motherless girl. I know Miss Rivers has done her best—but it's not the same thing. The second is that the child's desperately unhappy. You and I have had our ups and downs. Looking back over nearly fifty years I can recall some moments that I should be very sorry to have to live over again. But I don't think either of us have suffered as Lucy has during these last few days. Get that and you won't be too hard on her."

He paused. "Go on!" said Rivers hoarsely. "What are you trying to tell me? Go on!"

"When I came down here two weeks ago I saw that there was a screw loose somewhere. My room is next to Lucy's, and I heard her crying in the night. I persuaded her to confide in me. She told me that she and young Armour were in love with one another."

Rivers interrupted. "Impossible. They've never met."

"For several weeks before the—the death of Bertha Armour they had been meeting regularly two or three times a week in shelters along the Parade. The nights that you and Miss Rivers went out to play bridge."

"Are you—are you sure?" asked the Colonel.

"After her death they ceased to meet," continued Raynham, ignoring the interruption. "That was Armour's doing. He has been very anxious not to involve her in his family troubles. I believe him to be very deeply and sincerely attached to Lucy. I believe that, if necessary, he would die for her. He's not as black as he's been painted, John."

Rivers exploded. "A wastrel and scallywag. A fellow who was kicked out of his father's house for an offence that would have meant penal servitude if he'd been prosecuted, and who's earned his living since by sponging on silly old women, and is more than suspected of poisoning his sister. And you think him a suitable husband for my daughter? Or—perhaps there was no question of marriage? One never knows nowadays."

Raynham kept his temper. His brother-in-law's outburst was natural and excusable. "I shouldn't have chosen him for Lucy. I suppose you've seen to it that she met any eligibles that happen to be about?"

The Colonel stared. "Eligibles? What do you expect? If you mean have I encouraged any of the local cubs to come yapping round here, I haven't. I don't approve of the young men of to-day. No manners and a perpetual thirst."

"But you kept Lucy at home with nothing particular to do and expected her to be satisfied. It might have been all right if she'd been under-vitalized, but she isn't. She's Janet's daughter. Janet was twenty-eight when you married her, but there had been channels for her superfluous energy. She'd held down a difficult job and travelled a good bit. I don't want to rub it in, John, but if you don't fit a machine with a safety valve there's bound to be an explosion."

"Well—you may be right," said Rivers in a flat voice. "I think I should have been told before now though."

"I'm sorry about that," said Raynham. "I couldn't speak without her leave and she was afraid to tell you."

"Afraid? My little girl? She's never had an unkind word from me."

"She was afraid of hurting you," explained Raynham. "The question now is what are you going to do about it?"

The Colonel sighed. He looked unusually small and shrivelled as he sat there huddled in his dressing-gown. "Do—"

To give him time Raynham got up and drew back the curtains letting the cold grey light of dawn into the room. There was a clattering of milk carts down the road. One of the daily maids coming up the path glanced curiously at the window. Raynham switched off the electric light.

Rivers was speaking. "The fellow's younger sister and the gardener are coming before the Bench this morning. I can't be there under the circumstances. We'd better shut up the house and go away for a bit. Yes, that will be the best thing."

Raynham shook his head. "You won't get Lucy to agree to that."

"You mean that she intends to stick to this man?"

"Yes."

"Good Heavens! I heard yesterday that the latest theory of the police is that the brother and sister were in it, together with Lee, and that Brisling had a warrant ready for Armour's arrest. You're in with Brisling. He wouldn't have moved if he hadn't a pretty good case."

"He has," said Raynham. "If I were in his place I should put those three in the dock together and await a verdict of guilty with the utmost confidence. The motive, the means, the opportunity. There doesn't seem to be one weak link in the chain. I've made some investigations on my own and I've got a man working on the case, a queer little chap called Glide who's supposed to be very clever. For Lucy's sake I've done my utmost. But I'll admit to you that I haven't much hope."

His tone betrayed the dejection he had striven to hide until then.

He added in a still lower voice. "Sometimes—I have none."

He got up stiffly. "'Don't mind me. I'm dirty and unshaven. That's bad for the morale. What's that!"

The telephone bell was ringing in the hall. Raynham dashed out to it and snatched up the receiver.

"Sorry, John. I think it may be for me. Hallo . . . ! hallo . . . !"

Rivers, watching his face, sat down on the hall chair. He did not feel equal to another shock. "What is it?" he quavered.

Raynham motioned to him to be silent.

Chapter XXVIII

A SHOE FOR LUCK

Superintendent Brisling was tired. He had had a long and harassing day and there was more worry and responsibility to come. He ate a light supper, smoked a pipe afterwards and read a few pages of his favourite author, who was not, as might have been expected, Edgar Wallace, but Jane Austen. The immortal Jane calmed his nerves. He went to bed and to sleep.

He had not long dozed off when he was awakened by a knocking at the house door. He got up hastily and opened the window.

"Who's that?"

As his eyes grew accustomed to the darkness he discerned the stalwart figure of one of his subordinates. "Is it Evans?"

"Yes, sir. I reported what I'd seen this evening to the inspector, and he thought I'd better let you know. It's Armour. He's bolted."

"Bolted! How? The station's watched and the people who hire out cars have been warned." The superintendent became conscious of the undesirability of carrying on the conversation at the top of their voices, and of the inadequacy of his pyjamas to keep out the cold night air. "Wait!" he said. "I'll be down in five minutes."

In less than that time he had joined Evans on the doorstep. "Now let's have it. Come into my sitting-room. It's chilly here."

The constable told his story. His beat led him over the railway bridge as far as the cross-roads half a mile farther on. Shortly after six o'clock he had observed a large saloon car coming out of the White House grounds. It was lit inside and he had seen a bearded man in the back seat with a nurse in uniform. There was a gentleman who looked like a doctor in front sitting by the chauffeur.

Brisling nodded. "That's right. George Armour has been removed to the house of a doctor who takes M.D.s. O.K. so far, Evans, though of course you were quite right to notice and report it. Ramsay arranged that. He's the

Armours' family solicitor. He's been remiss. He ought to have been looking after them from the first. Well, never mind that. Go on."

Evans continued. He had been returning from the cross-roads about an hour later when he saw another car waiting outside the White House gates. A woman came out of the drive and entered the car. Two men followed after a short interval and the car was driven off. One of the men was Mark Armour. He had walked round in front of the car and had been clearly visible in the light of the head-lamps.

Brisling grunted. "It sounds like a get-away. Why the hell didn't you give the alarm at once? You could have gone to Doctor Cardew and rung us up from there."

"I thought it was all right, Superintendent, seeing that the gentleman who was driving was a friend of yours."

"A friend of mine?"

"Mr. Raynham, who's been staying along with Colonel Rivers. I saw the number of the car as it passed me. It was his. No mistake about that. It's been standing in the station yard most days lately."

"Raynham?" The superintendent was puzzled. He had trusted Raynham. He did not think that the brother-in-law of Colonel Rivers would assist a suspected person to escape arrest. He must know that if he did it would mean the end of his own career in the Service. No; there must be some other explanation.

"The woman?" he said, pondering.

"That must have been the other sister, sir. Her they call Winnie," said Evans. "When I passed the house for the last time before coming off duty I thought I'd better just have a look round so I went up the drive and flashed my lamp at the windows just to see if they were properly fastened. There was one on the left of the porch open at the top, and that gave me the excuse to knock and ring the bell, it being a part of our duties to warn householders if a ground-floor window is left open."

"Quite," said Brisling. "Were they duly grateful?"

"Nobody came, sir, and it was all dark. They must have heard me if there'd been anybody there. I thought, 'Well, they haven't come back!' and I began to feel worried. So as soon as I got back to the station I told the inspector and he said I'd better come on to you."

Brisling rubbed his chin reflectively. "Just so. But I don't see what we can do at this hour of the night."

"Oh! Beg pardon, sir, for interrupting, but the inspector said the party who'd been to see you with Mr. Raynham—the little man—called after you'd gone to-night and wrote a note to be delivered to you with this parcel, so I brought it along."

He laid a small brown paper parcel down on the table. The superintendent read the note. It was very short.

"My Dear Superintendent,

"This isn't a wedding, but old shoes are always supposed to bring luck. The one I am sending you herewith belongs to Miss Winifred Armour. Take note of the size.

"Yours faithfully,

"Hermann Glide."

"Hell!" said the superintendent. He tore the brown paper in his haste. He took up the flimsy, high-heeled, black kid slipper and turned it over. The size was stamped in gilt letters inside the sole. Four. What a fool he had been not to think of that possibility. The defence would make the most of the fact that the footprint outside the kitchen window of the house on Marine Parade might as well have been Winnie's as her younger sister's. But what else was there to connect her with the crime? Nothing that he knew of. But if she had actually bolted with her brother? Brisling found himself hoping that she had. "That will mean that the whole family were in it, barring George, and they can stand their trial together," he thought. He felt unusually savage, foreseeing that he might be blamed for not keeping a closer watch on the house. "She'll be detained during His Majesty's pleasure, and the other three will be hanged, and a good riddance of bad rubbish." Aloud he said.

"All right, Evans. Go back to the station and tell the inspector I'll go to the White House myself early to-morrow morning and take a search warrant. I'll take Collins and Sturt with me. They can bring the car round and pick me up here at six o'clock sharp. Is that clear?"

Evans saluted. "Yes, sir."

The superintendent went back to bed.

CHAPTER XXIX
THE WAY

MARK HAD NOT a latch-key. He might enter the house by way of the study window, or ring the bell and wait for Winnie to come down and admit him. But he had not reached the house when he heard a car stop at the gate and footsteps coming up the drive behind him. He waited and saw three burly men bearing down on him through the raw mist of the winter dawn. The police already.

"Is that you, Mr. Armour?"

"Yes. Good morning, Superintendent. You're bright and early."

"So are you. At least"—Brisling amended after switching on his pocket torch—"not bright. You look done up."

"I am. Do you mind turning that thing off me. It dazzles my eyes. Thanks."

They walked up the drive together, the two constables following.

"Where is your sister, Mr. Armour?"

"Haven't you got her?"

"I mean Miss Winifred."

"In bed and asleep, I imagine, at this hour."

"I advise you not to take that tone with me," said Brisling, sternly. "We know that she went away with you last night in Mr. Raynham's car."

"You're wrong," said Mark wearily. "Raynham took me up to Town to see my mother, who was dying, and he brought me back just now. You must have passed his car as you came along. You'll find Winnie here if you want her."

Brisling did not answer immediately. He was thinking hard. Evans had seen a woman. "We shall soon know," he said. They were come to the door. "Have you a key?"

"No."

Brisling rang the bell and followed that up with a thundering knocking. There was no sound or movement within.

"How do you get in usually, Mr. Armour?"

"There are two latch-keys. I forgot to take one last night. I daresay I could lift the catch of the study window."

Brisling nodded. They went round to the back of the house. Mark uttered an exclamation. The study window stood open. Brisling's face hardened. "Sturt," he said sharply, "stay here with Mr. Armour. Collins, you come with me. There's something wrong here."

"Why shouldn't I come in?" asked Mark irritably. He was sick of Brisling.

The superintendent stopped him. "We found you half way up the drive. How do we know if you were going up to the house—or coming away from it? You were facing towards the gate when we saw you. I make no charge—but if there's anything amiss here, Mr. Armour, I shall hold you."

"Oh—go to hell!" said Mark.

He remained on the path outside with one of the constables, while the other followed his superior officer into the study by way of the open window.

Brisling, puzzled and very much on the alert, went from room to room, drawing back curtains and pulling up blinds to admit the first faint glimmer of dawn. If Winifred Armour was upstairs why didn't she show herself? He went up and rapped at the door of her bedroom. There was no reply. He turned the handle and went in. He saw at once that the bed had not been slept in. The counterpane was still littered with scraps of ribbon and artificial flowers. There were a number of loose sheets of paper covered with scrawled and blotted writing on the little rosewood bureau. Some of it seemed to be poetry. Many words had been scratched out or written over. Brisling read a sentence here and there, and stiffened to attention:

The fiend voices rave—then a light—then thy breast— Oh, how could you be so cruel! Is my love such a worthless thing! After all I did and dared for your sake. They'd laugh at me if they knew. They did before. They won't again because I've finished. The long day is done and I am for the dark. I don't repent. She found a letter I had writ-

ten to you and hadn't posted. She said you'd written to her to complain of me. I won't believe that even now. She lied. I went to see you but you were out. Then it came into my mind what I might do. I was lucky to find the right bottle in the dispensary. I took just a little in one of the empty medicine bottles that were standing on the table waiting to be filled with your prescriptions. It was too large to be carried about much so I hunted about at home and found a little aspirin bottle in Mark's room that was just right. I threw that bottle away when I'd poured the stuff into her milk. There was some left in the big bottle. I buried it in the garden and dug it up again when Emily became troublesome. Is this what they call a confession? You must burn it when you've read it, darling, and never breathe a word. I'm telling you just to show you what I've done for you. They think it was the others—all but the little man who came last night when I was too miserable to think what I was saying. I hope I didn't admit too much to him. I can't remember. He frightened me rather, especially something he said when he went on about Cain and Abel. But God didn't do anything to Cain really. A brand isn't anything. Of course we all hated Bertha, and it might as well have been the others. They ought to be thankful to me for being brave enough. It won't do them any harm to be kept in prison. They think too much of themselves. But that man frightened me. I won't stay here to be taken and put away. She threatened me with that. There's a way. I've thought of it when the house shook. Oh God! There's somebody knocking at the door now—

Brisling read slowly and with difficulty, for the blots were frequent and several words almost illegible. "I suppose she was crying," he thought, "and tears dropping on the paper."

The constable who had been looking into the other rooms on that floor and overhead came back at that moment.

"There's nobody in the house, sir," he reported.

His superior gazed at him in a manner that showed that his thoughts were elsewhere. *There's a way. I've thought of it when the house shook.* He rushed to the window, threw it open and leaned out. Mark Armour and the other constable were waiting on the path below, but he had no eyes for them. He was looking at the lawn. Yes, there were footprints crossing it plainly visible on the wet grass. A single line of footprints going away from the house, and none returning. He looked at his watch.

"When's the first train from the junction?"

"Six-fifty," said Collins. "She's nearly due."

Brisling leaned further out of the window and shouted to the men below. His face was white. "She's gone that way!" he waved his arms. "The railway cutting. Hurry! There's only three minutes."

The constable was the slowest of comprehension. Mark was half way across the lawn before he understood what was expected of him.

Then he said "Coo!" and plunged in pursuit.

Brisling hurled himself down the stairs, with Collins close at his heels. They sprinted across the lawn after the others and down the long path between currant bushes and cucumber frames to the privet hedge at the bottom of the garden. Brisling pushed his way through a gap and found himself at the top of the railway embankment.

The line at this point passed through a deep cutting spanned by the railway bridge. The sides were as steep as the roof of a house. Mark was half way down, scrambling on his hands and knees. Constable Sturt, hampered by his clumsy service boots, was following more slowly. There was something that looked like a bundle of clothes below, lying across the shining steel rails.

"Shall I go too, sir?" asked Collins.

"No. Wait a bit. You'd only be kicking dirt into Sturt's eyes. The signals are down. There's no time."

"I can hear the train!" cried Collins. "Can't we do anything!"

Both men were violently agitated.

"If we had a rope"—Brisling's eyes were fixed on the two crouching figures, crawling laboriously down the slippery grass slope.

"Careful! Careful now!" he muttered. "Oh, my God!"

The young constable, standing beside him, screamed like a woman and covered his face with his hands.

Mark Armour had slipped. He made a desperate attempt to recover his balance, clutching at the short turf, but it was in vain. His body rolled down the slope on to the permanent way as the train came round the curve and passed through the cutting with a crash and a roar.

Slowly the clouds of steam from the engine eddied away. Constable Sturt, who had been lying spread-eagled on the bank, with his face buried in the grass, lifted his head, looked down once, and resumed his efforts. Brisling swallowed once or twice. He was still very pale. The bundle of clothes that had been lying across the rails had an oddly scattered appearance.

"Thank the Lord I'm short sighted," said Brisling.

Collins pointed a shaking finger at the second bundle lying between the rails a few feet farther down the permanent way.

"That's him," he said unsteadily. "Murderer or not, he gave his life—"

"He wasn't a murderer," said Brisling. "Poor devil!" He clutched his subordinate's arm in his excitement. "Look!" his voice cracked. The prone figure had struggled to its knees and then to its feet. It moved forward blindly, stumbling over the sleepers. "The train went over him and never touched him. He must have lain clear of the rails. Go back to the car, Collins, and drive to the station. We shall want the doctor and the ambulance. Tell them. I must go down the cutting."

"Mind you don't slip," said the younger man anxiously.

"It won't matter much if I do now," said Brisling grimly. "There won't be another train for an hour yet. I'd like to prevent him from turning round and seeing what's behind him. What's he doing now?" The wavering figure had tripped and fallen and was lying still.

"Fainted, by the look of it," said Collins, "and no wonder." He went off while the superintendent, who was not as young as he had been, commenced the descent of the embankment. Half way down he stopped to rest, breathing heavily, conscious of creaking joints, and his tight uniform collar. Glancing up he saw the police car driven by Collins crossing the bridge. A few months from now the bank he sat on would be thick with primroses. He had often seen them from the train. There was one rather untimely bud growing just by his hand. He observed it gratefully. It helped him somehow to face the horror that awaited him below.

Well, it was her own choice, and better, perhaps, than the slow, inexorable processes of the law.

The constable who had preceded him was waiting to help him down the last few feet, which were faced with brickwork, on to the permanent way.

"A nasty shock for you, Sturt," said the superintendent kindly. He stepped carefully over the rails. "Leave her," he added. "Look to the living. I'd rather he didn't come to himself until we've got him away from here," he added as he bent and wiped a smear of blood from the dark, unconscious face with an unexpected gentleness.

"He was brave," said Sturt. He shuddered. "He fell right in front of the train. I thought he'd be cut to pieces."

"Luck!" said Brisling. "Or perhaps—Shakespeare said something else. Have you read *Hamlet*, Sturt? You should. Well shaped or rough hewn, this looks like the end of the Armour case."

Chapter XXX
THE LAST

Hermann Glide's secretary took the visitor's card in to her employer and came back at once.

"Mr. Glide will be pleased to see you."

Glide left his desk to greet Geoffrey Raynham.

"No more trouble, I hope?" he said as they shook hands.

Raynham explained that he was leaving England, sailing for Singapore *en route* for another unnamed destination, on the morrow, and that he had come to say goodbye. "You mustn't think I don't realise how much we owe you," he said. "If it hadn't been for your shock tactics I doubt if Winifred Armour would have betrayed herself. Brisling thinks she'd have let the other three hang without batting an eyelash. There's a queer streak of callousness in these unbalanced neurotic people who are always so uncommonly sorry for themselves."

"I shouldn't wonder," said the little man placidly.

"And if the policeman on the beat hadn't knocked at the door when he did she'd probably have burnt that confession of hers. She thought they were coming to arrest her and chose a quicker end."

"Simla's for sale," said Raynham. "My brother-in-law has taken a house at Cheltenham and is living there with Miss Rivers. They have joined a bridge club and seem quite happy. My niece is in London taking a course in child welfare."

"Then she hasn't—she isn't"—began Glide.

"Mark Armour has gone out to Ceylon," said Raynham. "I got him a post on a plantation there. He'll be able to marry at the end of a year if he's run straight meanwhile and Lucy is still of the same mind. I thought a period of probation advisable." He smiled. "I believe they write to each other every day."

"And his sister—Claire Armour?"

"She married Lee. I got him a job, too, in the north of England. They'll be all right, I fancy." He paused. "When did you begin to suspect Winifred? I've often wondered."

Glide grinned. "About the time Superintendent Brisling began to suspect Claire. But—as you said just now, there wasn't an atom of evidence—without her confession. With it—you know the police dug all over the garden and found the bottle she'd buried with a few drops of liquid death still in it?"

"There's one point that will never be cleared up," said Raynham. "How did the arsenic get into the untouched cup of cocoa?"

"That's easy," said the little detective. "Winifred probably fancied that the cook knew more than she actually did and decided that she must be silenced before she gave her evidence at the inquest. So she went after dark to call on Emily with her useful bottle of—silencer—in her handbag. She chose the back way because she didn't want to attract the attention of the neighbours. When she arrived she heard raised voices, and, peeping through the scullery window, saw Emily and Lee having the row he told us about. He rushed out of the house without noticing the eavesdropper. Now the rest is conjecture. Emily left the kitchen for a minute, and Winifred took the opportunity to slip in and pour some of the mixture as before into the cup. Naturally she assumed that when Emily came back she'd drink her cocoa. I expect she went home quite pleased with her evening's work. But, as you know, what actually happened was rather different. Emily's heart didn't stand the strain of the quarrel with Lee, and she died a natural death."

"Near enough," said Raynham. "Well—I'm glad I got my leave this year." He stood up. "For Lucy—"

His sunburned and sinewy hand engulfed the fragile little claw.

Glide blinked up at him. "I've got it down on my files," he said, "as the Case of the Good Uncle."

THE END